"Your beliefs are of no moment, my lord."

Meg's voice was icy as she stiffened with indignation.

"Good," Wrendale said and held her more firmly lest they not enjoy their waltz.

"For instance," he continued, smiling down at her, "looking at you, it is easy to see only your beauty, while others might ignore the temper indicated by that pugnacious little chin."

"That is not your affair," Meg said angrily. "Or do you feel that you have as much right to interfere in my life as you apparently do in everyone else's?"

"If I have interfered, as you put it, in your life, you should be glad of it," he answered smoothly.

Meg could feel colour rising in her cheeks. "You are the most ill-mannered, insufferable...! I'll not stay and be insulted by you any further, my lord."

She wrenched herself out of his arms and strode off the floor, leaving Lord Wrendale standing alone, scandalized, in the midst of the dancers.

THE CYNIC

ELIZABETH MICHAELS

Harlequin Books

TORONTO • NEW YORK • LONDON
AMSTERDAM • PARIS • SYDNEY • HAMBURG
STOCKHOLM • ATHENS • TOKYO • MILAN
MADRID • WARSAW • BUDAPEST • AUCKLAND

For J. and M.

Published October 1992

ISBN 0-373-31183-4

THE CYNIC

PROLOGUE

A WHISPER SWEPT THROUGH the crowded ballroom. Heads turned; ladies tried their best to appear nonchalant, shading curious eyes with fans and posies of flowers, while positioning themselves for the most advantageous view of the double doors which led into the room. Gentlemen, less constrained by the demands of good manners, frankly stared, craning their necks to get a better look at the entrance. One young buck went so far as to climb on top of one of the gilt chairs which lined the walls of the elegant chamber, but it was generally agreed, later, that he had gone beyond the pale. The whisper became a murmur, then a buzz. Finally, when it seemed as though every head in the room was turned in that direction, a footman stepped into the doorway and cleared his throat. "My Lady Carstairs." He paused before adding, in a voice which showed clearly his enjoyment of his momentous task, "And Miss Margaret Sutton!" A sigh escaped several hundred throats at once.

Across the ballroom, Richard Trevore, Earl of Wrendale, cocked one elegant eyebrow in the direction of the crowd. "What ho?" he asked. "Has a Royal actually chosen to grace this humble gathering?"

His companion, a lady well into her seventies clad in a hideous demi-robe of purple sarcenet, cackled.

"Lord, no," she said. "No one would make such a fuss about a mere Royal. No, my dear, 'tis the Season's latest, and by far richest, young heiress."

"Surely not?" Wrendale said. "Heiresses are not so rare as all that."

"No, but neither are they so rich," the lady said bluntly. She leaned forward. "This Miss Sutton," she told Wrendale confidentially, "is supposed to have in excess of twenty thousand pounds...a year! She's fresh on the Town and assumed to be on the catch for a husband. No father, either—he died last year. You must have heard of Miser Sutton? Well, this gal's his daughter. She's in the care of that fool, Sally Carstairs."

"So Miss Sutton is an heiress?" said Wrendale. "That would explain it, then. I suppose we should be glad that the young lady was not actually mobbed as she stepped in the door."

"They don't call you 'the Cynic' for naught, do they?" Lady Buckham remarked. "It's what one so especially likes about you, Wrendale; you may be the rudest man in London, but you always tell the truth, and no bones about it." She nodded towards the door. "'Tis quite lowering," she said, "that one young chit should have so much—I call it positively nauseating." Wrendale chuckled, and the old lady cackled again. "Which ain't to say," she added, "that I wouldn't try to buckle her to my boy, if he weren't already married and father to children as old as she is. But there is no point in repining, is there?"

"Too true," said Wrendale. He swept his companion a deep bow. "What one particularly admires about you, Lady Buckham, is that you so exactly understand the realities of life."

"Get along with you," Lady Buckham advised him. "I know you won't be chasing after this gal, on account of having more blunt than you know how to spend already, but you must have something better to do than waste your time with a dried-up old piece like me. Go and enjoy yourself, boy! For myself, I shall go and meet the chit. Curiosity is a curse, ain't it, Wrendale?"

Wrendale bowed and left his friend, while reflecting ruefully that only someone of Lady Buckham's advanced years could still call him "boy." He was a man just turned forty, though the years had dealt very kindly with him. At his temples his black hair was barely touched with grey; his face was almost unlined, and the erect carriage of his tall frame would put to shame many a gentleman twenty years his junior. Only his blue eyes hinted at his true age; they stared out at the world with a weary, cosmopolitan knowledge which gave credence to his nickname.

Wrendale strolled away from Lady Buckham, carefully avoiding the knot of people gathered round the newest arrival at the ball. He nodded to a friend or two, spoke briefly to a sophisticated lady who had once enjoyed his protection, then wandered out the French doors at the end of the room to the terrace. The night was beautiful, in the way which only a perfect night in spring can be. Wrendale looked up at the moon for a moment, raising his quizzing glass with a gesture which would have depressed the pretensions of any human so observed. Then he lit a cheroot and turned his back on the bright moonlight which flooded the garden.

Lord Wrendale was not, in the general way of things, easily bored. Though a confessed cynic who found the schemes and machinations of his fellow man ineffably wearisome, he normally took pleasure in the order and entertainments of his life. But of late this contentment had begun to lessen. Wrendale could not quite determine why this was so; his popularity was as great as ever, the fortune he had inherited at the tender age of twenty had, if anything, increased under his shrewd management, and his love life, despite his current lack of a mistress, was more than satisfactory. None the less, Wrendale was beginning to find his life tedious. He found himself restless when in the country, dissatisfied when in London. A quick trip to Paris, from which he had just returned, had been a waste of both time and money; even that incomparable city had not succeeded in eradicating his feeling of ennui. And the thought of the upcoming Season did nothing to lift his spirits—he had gone the round of balls and routs, drums and alfresco breakfasts once too often, he supposed. He had begun to wonder, half humourously, if he were in need of a strong physick.

Wrendale looked at his pocket watch and realized that an hour had passed. He relit his cheroot and turned again to stare out over the moon-bright garden. A sound caught his attention; he looked along the path which ran through the shrubs and flower beds and could barely discern, on a secluded bench, a pair of figures, male and female.

"Pray do not be absurd," the woman said. By her voice, Wrendale guessed her to be fairly young. "It cannot be so."

"But you have captured my heart!" the man exclaimed, his voice carrying clearly in the still air. "The moment I saw you I knew that you were the one lady with whom I could live happily for the rest of my days."

"We have only just met," the young lady protested. "Scarcely more than an hour ago we were complete strangers."

"Do you not believe in love at first sight?" the man asked.

"No, I do not." Wrendale chuckled to himself at the girl's damping tone.

The young man plunged on. "It was written in the stars," he said grandly. "You must be my bride!"

Wrendale sensed, rather than heard, the girl's exasperated sigh. "I shall never marry," she said clearly. "But even if I intended to, I would not become betrothed to a gentleman I'd known for less than an evening!"

It was quite clear that the wooing was not proceeding at all according to the young gentleman's plan. He stiffened, every line of his body proclaiming his outraged pride. As he began to speak again, the young woman rose to her feet and began to move off down the path. As she stepped into a pool of moonlight, Wrendale saw that she was not quite so young as he had imagined by the sound of her voice, perhaps twenty-four or twenty-five. She was very lovely, he thought dispassionately. Small and fine-boned, she moved with an unselfconscious pride, her well-shaped head carried high. Her hair was a rich auburn shade and curled about her head in a cap of ringlets. Only her chin, Wrendale thought, detracted from her look of fragile helplessness; it thrust forward aggressively, lending character to a face which otherwise might have been just a touch insipid.

The young woman's importunate suitor was not to be so lightly dismissed. He came up to the woman and caught her arm. As the man stepped into the light, Wrendale recognized a young buck about Town, one Fortesque by name, well known to be expensive and ruinously improvident. "You cannot leave me so," Fortesque said.

The young woman tried to disentangle her arm. "I have no wish to be uncivil," she said, "but—"

"I will have you, or die trying!" young Fortesque cried dramatically. With this, he swept her up in his arms, ignoring her protests.

Wrendale took one last puff of his cheroot, flipped it off into the gardens and strode down the terrace steps. Three strides brought him to the struggling pair; he tapped Mr. Fortesque on the shoulder.

"Damn you for your impudence," the young man growled, whirling round. The moonlight was enough to illuminate his sudden pallour. "Oh! My lord Wrendale," he stammered. "Can I . . . that is to say, may I . . . ?"

"You may," Wrendale said politely. "Good evening."

"I—I . . . of course," Fortesque said lamely. With a muttered, "Your servant, ma'am," he was gone.

The young lady turned to Wrendale, her eyes flashing. "Have you ever seen anything so absurd?" she exclaimed. "To profess undying love, and on an hour's acquaintance, if you please! 'Tis the most ridiculous thing I have ever heard."

"Quite," Wrendale said coolly. "One should be acquainted for at least a fortnight before making such an extravagant claim, don't you agree?"

She gave a trill of laughter. "At least," she said. Wrendale offered her his arm and they began to move back towards the terrace.

"Which is not to say," Wrendale continued, "that you are not partially to blame."

"I beg your pardon?"

"If you will go walking in moonlit gardens with impetuous young men, then you must expect to be made love to," he said.

The girl stopped. She turned to face Wrendale. "Forgive me, but what concern is it of yours?" she asked. Her tone was icy.

"None whatsoever," Wrendale admitted calmly. "But, as I might not be here to rescue you the next time, I thought I might just mention the imprudence of flouting convention. It has its uses, you know; it protects naïve young ladies from the consequences of their ignorance."

The young lady appeared to be struggling to control her temper. "I am neither naïve nor ignorant, sir."

"If that is the case, then I must admit to a certain puzzlement," Wrendale said. "If you are not naïve, and not on the catch for a husband—"

"I most certainly am not!" the girl said.

"Then I fail to see the point of this little moonlight excursion," he said.

"The desire for a breath of fresh air was my only reason for accompanying Mr. Fortesque," the girl said stiffly.

"Thereby proving your naïvety," Wrendale said. "You had best have a care, my dear, lest you find yourself forced to wed a fool like Fortesque, only through a lack of regard for convention. I fear you would find such as he a poor bargain indeed."

"You are intolerable, sir," the girl said, teeth clenched. "I vow, I prefer the outright offences of Mr. Fortesque to yours, cloaked as they are in a false courtesy."

"Oh, I never trouble myself with courtesy," Wrendale said. "I'm known for it, in fact—my rudeness, that is."

"I see," the young woman said tightly. "And untroubled by that fact, apparently. But it follows, doesn't it? A gentleman may behave as he wishes and not be thought remarkable." She was furious; her chin jutted forward pugnaciously. "It is only we weakwilled women who must toe the line of convention."

Wrendale shrugged. "The world is what it is," he said.

"Your world, perhaps," she said. "Not mine."

"I fear that you will find the ton sadly intolerant of free thinking." He smiled at her.

The young woman drew herself up. "I thank you for your escort, sir," she said stiffly. "Good evening." With that, she turned and marched back into the ballroom.

Wrendale watched her retreating back and chuckled. Perhaps, he thought, the Season would not be quite so dull after all!

CHAPTER ONE

LADY SALLY CARSTAIRS let the pile of invitations and calling cards fall through her fingers. "You are off to an excellent start, my love," she said cheerfully. "It seems that everyone in Town knows of your arrival, and welcomes it. 'Tis most gratifying." Lady Carstairs was a large, somewhat untidy-looking woman. Her grey hair was constantly on the verge of total disorder; however hard her dresser worked to arrange it, within minutes it was always pulled about her head as though she had been out in a strong wind. Her taste in clothing, running as it did to frills and furbelows, was most unfortunate for a woman of her girth.

Margaret Sutton made no response; she stared out the breakfast-room window, her thoughts clearly far away.

"Of course, it was only to be expected," Lady Carstairs continued. "With your fortune, it was a foregone conclusion that the world would beat a path to your door." She regarded Meg thoughtfully. "Which is not to say," she continued, "that you must not be careful to demonstrate the niceties of behaviour. A lady's reputation is her most important asset, my sweet."

Meg frowned. "What do you mean?"

Lady Carstairs began to toy with her teacup. "I could not help but notice that you disappeared for a time last evening, and that you left with that awful Fortesque person. If I noticed, Meg, you may be sure that others did, as well. It was ill-considered, my pet; nothing is more fatal to a lady's chances than to be judged fast.''

"This makes no sense!" Meg exclaimed. "On the one hand, I have been warned time and time again that I must beware, that every young man in London will be after me for my fortune. Now you say that I must be careful to guard my reputation. Which is it, Aunt? Am I to be valued only for the sake of my purse, or is my fair name the coin which will buy me a husband?''

"The rules of Polite Society—" Lady Carstairs began.

"Bah! I'm sick to death of rules," Meg cried. "My father kept me isolated on our estate, refusing to allow me to go out into Society for fear that some fortune-hunter would steal me away. It took his death to release me from my prison.''

"Meg!" Lady Carstairs gasped. "How can you speak of your father so?''

"Can you deny that I would have been prevented from making my come-out if he were still alive?" Meg demanded.

Meg's father, the late Thomas Sutton, known as "Miser" Sutton, had been a tight-fisted, cold-hearted recluse, horrified by the thought that his beautiful daughter might be wooed for her money. As a result, however much Lady Carstairs, the closest friend of Meg's long-deceased mother, had protested, nothing would convince the older man that he should allow Meg her come-out. It was not until after Thomas's death that Meg had been able to join Sally Carstairs in London.

"And now," Meg continued, "now, when I finally have my freedom, you tell me that I must not do this and I must not do that. Well, I refuse! I have waited a long time to come to Town, and I am quite, quite determined to enjoy myself, whatever anyone may say."

"No one wishes to deny you your enjoyment, Meg," Lady Carstairs said. "Lord knows, I tried time and time again to convince your father not to keep you so close. That is neither here nor there; I will not speak ill of the dead. But, my dear," she leaned forward, "it would be fatal for you to assume that you are above the standards of Polite Society. Your fortune is great, that is true, but it will not excuse all."

"I daresay that it will excuse a great deal, though," Meg said drily.

"Not among the best people," Lady Carstairs responded. She regarded her charge unhappily. "Do you not want to find a husband?"

"Not at all," Meg said briskly. "I have been too long in thrall to my father to willingly place myself in another man's sway."

Sally Carstairs sighed. Fool she might be, but she knew better than to argue with Meg when the girl's jaw was set in that particular way. "Well," she said practically, "you'll find it difficult indeed to enjoy yourself if you're not received by the ton. And you won't be, Meg, if you do not have a care for your behaviour." She regarded Meg earnestly. "You just don't know, my dear, how many pitfalls lie in wait for the unwary young lady in London."

Meg wavered for a moment, then capitulated. "Very well, Aunt Sally," she said. "Tell me what I must not do."

"Well," Lady Carstairs said, "'tis difficult to know where to begin." She thought for a moment. "First of all, you must be terribly careful about being alone with a gentleman. I know it was the veriest innocence which made you stroll in the garden with Fortesque last evening, but really, Meg, it will not do."

"And how did you know that we were in the garden?" Meg asked, eyes twinkling.

"I, er, I looked," Sally Carstairs admitted. "After all, pet, you are my responsibility, you know. But I saw that Lord Wrendale was escorting you in, so I slipped away."

"I see," Meg said, all signs of amusement gone. "So it was very wrong of me to be alone with Mr. Fortesque, but perfectly all right for me to be private with this Lord Wrendale?"

"Oh, but my dear, the cases are completely different! Fortesque is a young ne'er-do-well, well known to be chasing after every heiress in Town, while Wrendale is...well, Wrendale! He is all one would wish for in a gentleman: rich, handsome and impeccably born."

"And as rude as can hold, by his own admission."

"Call it, rather, refreshingly honest," Sally Carstairs said.

Meg snorted, a most unladylike sound. "'Tis ironic," she said. "Mr. Fortesque was no more than tiresome last evening, however little you may think of him. But Wrendale, who is so very much your favourite, actually insulted me!"

"Nonsense," said Lady Carstairs dampingly. "He wouldn't do any such thing."

"Would he not?" Meg retorted. "He told me that it was my own fault if a gentleman stepped over the line. He said that if I would walk in the garden with impetuous young men, then I must expect to... to be made love to," she finished in a lower tone.

Lady Carstairs shrugged. "He has a point," she said.

"What? How can you take his side?" Meg cried. "He was insufferable! It was his behaviour which was unforgivable, not mine."

"None the less, it sounds as though he gave you good advice," Sally Carstairs said, "however disinclined you may be to take it." She looked thoughtful. "It was most kind of him to take such an interest in you," she said. "Perhaps," she added too casually, "perhaps we should invite him to dine, just as a thank you, so to speak."

"Oh, no, Aunt Sally," Meg said grimly. "Don't get that look in your eye. Not only do I not feel any attraction towards his lordship, I positively dislike him. And you may believe me when I tell you that the feeling is entirely mutual."

"But you will try, won't you, Meg?" Sally said. "To succeed in London? Which includes, I must warn you, getting along with Wrendale. He is too much the arbiter of Society to be flouted." She watched Meg anxiously.

"I'll try," Meg said. "I can't promise that I'll accomplish the thing, but I shall try."

JOHNNY TREVORE straightened his neckcloth, checked to make sure that his boots had picked up no trace of dust on the walk over, then rapped smartly on the door.

"Good morning, Stubbs," he said cheerfully to Lord Wrendale's butler. "My uncle in?"

"Good day, Master John," said Stubbs in sonorous tones. "His lordship is still abovestairs, dressing. May I see you into the study?"

"No need," said Johnny, moving past the butler and starting up the stairs two at a time. "I'm sure he won't mind if I join him."

"But, sir...!" Stubbs began; an insouciant wave was his only answer.

Johnny Trevore strolled into Lord Wrendale's room whistling. "Morning, Wren!" he called. "What's to do?"

Wrendale did not turn away from arranging his neckcloth at the mirror. "John," he nodded in greeting. "Did Stubbs send you up?"

His damping tone did not seem to affect his nephew. Johnny shook his head. "No, the old fussbudget tried to stop me; almost had an apoplexy, in fact, when he saw that I meant to join you. But I knew you wouldn't mind if I came up to bear you company while you dressed."

"As it happens," Wrendale said calmly, "I don't, but I daresay a great many other people might. Do you make a habit of bursting unannounced into your friends' dressing-rooms?"

"Of course not," Johnny said scornfully. "Think I'm as crude as all that? But you ain't a friend, are you? Mean to say, you're more than a friend, really...or different from a friend, I suppose, since we're related.... Oh, you know what I mean," he finished impatiently.

"I'm not at all sure that I do, but I'll take it as a compliment," Wrendale said. "This is a noteworthy occasion, young John; I don't recall when last I saw you abroad before noon."

"I haven't seen you for this age or more, so I thought I'd toddle over and say hello," Johnny said blithely. "Perhaps join you for breakfast?"

"Most assuredly," Wrendale said. He turned to his valet, who hovered behind Wrendale, a pile of crisp neckcloths held reverently over his arm. "Adam," Wrendale said, "pray go below and tell Stubbs that Master John will be joining me for breakfast, won't you?" The valet bowed, deposited the neckcloths gently in an armoire and departed.

Wrendale turned back to the mirror. He gave one final twitch to the cascade of starched linen at his throat, eyed it for a moment, then unerringly placed a sapphire stickpin in its folds. Johnny came and stood beside him, observing the finished result.

Johnny Trevore was as unlike Lord Wrendale in appearance as he was in temperament. He was short and somewhat stocky; his open countenance and eager expression were an exact reflection of his attitude towards life. The sandy hair which persisted in falling across his forehead was his constant despair, aspiring as he did to his uncle's easy elegance. Only Johnny's eyes, blue as cornflowers, testified to his relationship to the tall man who stood beside him.

"Deucedly fine way to tie a neckcloth, Wren," Johnny said. "Did you invent it?"

"I did," said Wrendale. "Do you like it?"

"I just said I did, didn't I?" Johnny said. "What do you call it?"

Wrendale regarded his handiwork dispassionately. "I do believe I shall call it the Trevore Fall," he said.

"Go it!" said Johnny enthusiastically. "Won't that bring a shine to the old family name, though?"

Wrendale cocked an eyebrow at his nephew. "One can only hope," he murmured, "that we have a trifle more to bring honour to our name than the arrangement of a neckcloth, however elegant it may be."

"We do," Johnny said, "but all those knights and earls and lords and that ancestor of ours who fought at Agincourt don't count for much today. It's a new age, don't you know."

Wrendale sighed. "Johnny," he said, "sometimes you make me feel as old as time itself."

Johnny made a rude noise. "Don't try to gammon me, Wren," he said. "You're the pink of the ton, slap up to the mark and complete to a shade. I only hope I've half your energy and style when . . ." He stopped.

"When you're my age?" Wrendale finished with a laugh. "Are you quite through insulting me, you abominable brat?"

Johnny looked crestfallen until he saw the affection in his uncle's eyes. "Well," he said, "I didn't plan to insult you."

"Of course you didn't," Wrendale said. "You never do. But somehow . . ."

"It just happens!" Johnny grinned at his uncle.

"Let's go down and eat," Wrendale said. "If I must deal with you so early in the day, at least let me have my sustenance first."

The two men made their way down the stairs and into the breakfast room. Wrendale waved Stubbs away; he and John served themselves from the dishes on the sideboard. For several minutes afterward they occupied themselves with their meals.

"So, John," Wrendale said finally. "What really brings you here this morning?"

"I've told you, Wren, I..." Johnny began. Wrendale met his nephew's gaze, the slightest of smiles lifting the corner of his mouth, "Dash it all, I never could lie to you," Johnny said ruefully.

"No, you never could," his uncle agreed. "What is it? Money?"

Johnny began to fidget with his serviette. "Well, actually, it is," he said all in a rush. "I've run a little short, and it's still a deuced long time until quarter day."

Wrendale continued to cut his breakfast sirloin. "How much do you need?" he asked.

"A pony would do nicely," Johnny said eagerly. "And of course I'll pay you back on quarter day; my mother's man is very good about settling up with me promptly."

"How is your mother?" Wrendale asked. "Does she know of your... temporary embarrassment?"

"Lord, no!" Johnny said. "Do you think I'd go running to her for the blunt, as if I were still a child? What kind of flat do you think me?"

"Not a flat at all," said Wrendale. "A bit green, perhaps, but no more than that." Taking out his pocket-book, he counted out a hundred pounds and pushed the pile of banknotes over to his nephew. "There," he said. "Never let it be said that I allowed my favourite nephew to end up pockets-to-let."

"You are a brick, Wren," said Johnny. "I knew I could count on you."

Wrendale leaned back in his chair. "Yes, you can," he said. "But I trust that my largesse gives me the right to offer you a bit of unsolicited advice?"

Johnny waved his coffee cup. "Have at it!"

"Give up the Billington woman, Johnny," Wrendale said. "She may well be the ruin of you if you don't."

Johnny flushed and rose to his feet. "My personal affairs are none of your concern," he said with dignity. "If you'll excuse me?" He left the money lying on the table.

"What happened to 'have at it'?" Wrendale asked. "Sit down, Johnny, do. You look the absolute fool."

His uncle's words had a quelling effect on the boy; he sat back down. "I said I'd listen, so I will," Johnny said sullenly. "But you are wasting your breath."

"I daresay I am. However, one can but try," Wrendale said. "Pray don't misunderstand me—I'm not saying that you shouldn't have a mistress, John. Any boy your age worth his salt has a mistress."

"Thank you so much," Johnny said sarcastically.

"But Patsy Billington is another matter altogether," Wrendale said. "Good God, boy, she has to be almost twice your age! And rather too experienced into the bargain."

"I resent you speaking of her that way," Johnny said stiffly. "She has been everything that is most kind to me."

"If you call it kindness," Wrendale said, "to drain a half-green lad of his last shilling."

"That's not the way it is at all," Johnny said hotly. "She never asks me for anything. Oh, she did agree that I should pay her living expenses, but she always scolds me if I try to give her a present. She was very cross with me for buying her a chaise and four. She didn't even want to accept it!" He stared accusingly at his uncle. "And I must say, Uncle," he stressed the word, "I find your attitude curious. You have a mistress every bit as expensive as Patsy!"

"As it happens, at the moment I do not. And in any event, the cases are a little different, don't you agree?" Wrendale said gently. "First of all, I'm not a green boy out on the Town for the first time. Secondly, I am in command of my own fortune, which you shall not be for another four years. Thirdly..." he said. "Thirdly, no one has ever whispered that I was thinking of marrying one of my paramours."

"Marriage?" Johnny exclaimed. "Dashed gossip-mongers will say anything, won't they? That's one notion which need not trouble you. I'm very fond of Patsy, but no more than that."

"I'm glad," said Wrendale. "But that does not set my mind totally at rest. It is more your heart I'm concerned about, Johnny, than anything else." He looked up at his nephew. "I've a great affection for you, halfling; I should hate to see you hurt."

The anger died out of Johnny's face. "I'm dashed fond of you, too, Wren," he said awkwardly. "And I appreciate your concern, I do. But you needn't worry. I've no intention of being hurt by la Billington or any other woman."

Lord Wrendale stifled a sigh. There, he thought, speaks a lad of great spirit and absolutely no sense!

"WHAT?" THE LADY reclining on the chaise lounge sat bolt upright. "What did you say?"

The overdressed woman sitting across from her tittered. "Really, my dear Lavinia, I would never have

mentioned the matter if I'd known that it would upset you so." The malice in her eyes gave the lie to her
words. "Particularly," she said, "as I know the delicate state of your health." She tittered again and took
a sip of her tea.

Lavinia Trevore swung her legs off the chaise. The
blond hair which had once been likened to spun gold
may have faded a bit and the glorious figure thick-
ened slightly, but Lavinia Trevore was still a most attractive woman. Her ill health was in truth no more
than an excuse for Lavinia to avoid visiting London,
a place she disliked, and a convenient reason to cry off
from any social engagement which she feared might
prove to be tedious.

"I don't believe it," she said flatly. "'Tis the merest gossip, I have no doubt." She fixed an accusing
glare on her neighbour, Lady Milland. "I take it very
ill, Serena, that you would pass on such nonsense,
when you must know that there's not an ounce of
truth in it."

Lady Milland shrugged. "That may be, I suppose," she said. "But really, my dear, all of London
is abuzz with the news. And I daresay we should not
be surprised; young men will have their straw damsels, will they not?" Lady Milland tried unsuccess-
fully to hide her enjoyment of her neighbour's
discomfiture. "Though by all accounts," she added
avidly, "this little misalliance goes far beyond the
bounds of youthful indiscretion."

Mrs. Trevore shook her head. "Not my John," she
said. "He couldn't be fool enough to develop a tendre
for that Billington woman; he would never so far forget himself. And Wrendale would not allow John to
lose his head, or to be entrapped by a fallen woman.

Whatever one may say about Wrendale, he would never ignore his duty to his only nephew."

"Oh, Wrendale!" Lady Milland said in a dismissing tone. "Gentlemen do view these things so very differently than we do, do they not? And to be perfectly honest, Lavinia, I've never thought Wrendale overly concerned with the niceties of civilized behaviour. He is well known to be the rudest man in London; he was once actually heard to say that he thought the Prince Regent an overblown roué. Such arrogance!"

Mrs. Trevore, who privately agreed with Wrendale about the Prince, kept the thought to herself "Rudeness is one thing, family duty another," she said. "Tell me again what it was that your son wrote to you."

"William said," Lady Milland told Lavinia, leaning forward in her seat, "that *tout le monde* is talking about John's pursuit of Patsy Billington. They say that John is beggaring himself to drown her in gifts; just last week, he bought her a new chaise and four." Mrs. Trevore, who knew to a crown what Johnny's allowance was, shuddered. "My son wrote that there is even some speculation," Lady Milland whispered, "that John may be thinking of offering the woman marriage." She sat back in her seat, satisfied.

"What absolute rubbish," Lavinia Trevore said. "My John may be young, but he is neither foolish nor unprincipled. He would never offer such a woman the protection of his name. William has let his imagination run away with him, I fear. If I may say so, Serena, your eldest son is sometimes less than sensible."

Lady Milland's eyes narrowed. "Pray do not blame William for your son's inexcusable behaviour," she said in an icy tone. "My William has never caused me a moment's worry, which, I'm sorry to say, is more than can be said of your John. Even as a boy John was wild and hot to hand."

Mrs. Trevore gasped with outrage. "That is not true!" she cried. "Johnny played his pranks as a child, I will allow, but only those that any child of spirit will play. William, on the other hand, has always been the colourless, tale-bearing gapeseed that he is now."

Lady Milland stood and drew herself up to her full height, which was not great. "I shall not stay," she said, "and listen to you insult William. I tried to do my Christian duty by coming and telling you what folly your son is engaged upon now. But I wash my hands of the matter. When you find yourself mother-in-law to a woman that is no better than the veriest trollop, Lavinia, you will be well served indeed!" With that, Lady Milland swept out of the room.

Lavinia Trevore rose from her chaise lounge. What cheek that Milland woman had, coming to her with such a tale! There couldn't be a word of truth to it; John would never be so foolish. Would he? Lavinia could not help but recall the stories she had heard from time to time of other young gentlemen and their falls from grace. She would never have imagined that her Johnny could cause her such worry, but she supposed that no mother ever did expect such a thing from her child.

And what of Wrendale? Lavinia had never been overly close to her brother-in-law; though they treated each other with respect, there had never been a bond of affection between Lavinia and her late husband's brother. But Wrendale was fond of Johnny, Lavinia knew. Indeed, she would have said that her son was the one creature on earth for whom Wrendale did care.

Surely he would put a stop to this unthinkable misalliance? Well, she did not propose to stand about and wait for Wrendale to save her son.

Lavinia tugged on the bell pull. When her butler answered the call she said, "Send Anna to me. We've a great deal to do, Ransom. I'm going to London!"

IT WAS FULL DAYLIGHT in Portman Square. The door of the elegant townhouse opened; two men emerged, escorted out by a yawning doorman. Through the double doors, beyond a marble foyer, a pair of baize-covered tables could be seen; several servants were sweeping and tidying what was clearly a gaming hell.

The two gentlemen blinked at the sunlight as they came out. The taller of the two, a thin, awkward-looking man who seemed to be all knees and elbows, raised his hand to summon a hackney cab. His companion shook his head.

"Let's walk," the handsome, almost pretty blond gentleman said. "'Twas woefully stuffy inside. The fresh air will do us both good, I have no doubt."

"True," the thin man said. "And it will save me the cost of a cab. Lord, what a drubbing I took this evening! My luck was most definitely out." The two men began to saunter down the street.

"It isn't a matter of luck," said Roger Marden. "You have the worst head for cards I've ever seen, yet you will insist on playing piquet, a game which is all finesse. It quite baffles me."

"That's easy for you to say," Willy Fortesque, the thin man, said. "You'd the devil's own luck this evening, as usual. How much did you win?"

"Five thousand pounds," Marden said complacently. "A tolerably rewarding night, I will allow."

Fortesque whistled. "Gad!" he said. "'Tis a fortune you've won. How can you always be pockets-to-let when you win your wagers so consistently? Particularly as you play for such dashed high stakes."

Marden shrugged. "I have expensive tastes, my lad," he said.

"Your high-flyers, no doubt," Fortesque said. "Are you still keeping that Billington woman?"

"Thankfully, no," said Marden with a delicate shudder. "An exquisite piece, I'll admit, but becoming a trifle shop-worn, I fear. No, I passed her on. That young fool Trevore has her under his protection, I believe."

The men had reached Marden's townhouse. They entered the small, perfectly appointed house. Marden's butler dozed on a chair in the entryway; the elderly man jumped to his feet as his master entered. Marden waved him away and escorted his guest into the study.

"Barton looked positively sick when you won that last hand," Fortesque said. "I hope he don't go home and put a period to his existence. He certainly seemed desperate enough to do it, and your reputation couldn't stand another one. Remember that Worthing youngster?"

Marden growled. "They shouldn't wager if they can't afford to lose," he said. "It's not my part to play nursemaid to young asses who don't know when to leave the table." He poured brandy and gave a glass to his friend.

Willy Fortesque tugged at his collar. "Ah, Marden . . ." he began. He stopped and cleared his throat. "Roger," he said in a more hearty voice. "Might you make me a small loan? Just until quarter day, you understand; I'll repay you then, with interest, of course."

Marden fixed him with a jaded eye. "Don't be ridiculous," he said. "It's difficult enough for me to afford my own small pleasures. I certainly can't afford to support you, too."

Fortesque sank back in his seat. "I don't know what I'll do," he said. "I'm at point non plus."

"You need a rich wife, old son," Marden said. "That would put everything to rights for you."

"I almost had one, last night," Fortesque said with a pout. "She was right in the palm of my hand. If it hadn't been for a bit of incredibly bad luck, I'd be betrothed right now to the richest girl in London, and on her first night in Town!"

Marden looked interested. "The Sutton chit?" he asked. He had heard talk of London's latest heiress—her fortune was rumoured to be enormous. "And you almost had her?" His tone was incredulous.

"I did," protested Fortesque. "If it weren't for that hound Wrendale, there would have been a notice in the Gazette this morning, announcing our engagement. The girl is ripe for the plucking, I tell you. She's as rich as can hold and too green to know her way about. She says she don't want to marry, but I pay no heed to that."

"What has Wrendale to say to the matter?" Marden watched his friend.

"Nothing, but that didn't stop him," Fortesque said gloomily. "He pushed his way into a private conversation and spirited the girl away without so much as a by your leave. I should have called him out."

Marden hooted. "You, call out the best marksman in London? Do be sensible, Willy. 'Twas your own fault, I have no doubt; you must have been plaguing the girl. You should have expected her friends to come to her aid.''

"That's the worst part," Fortesque said. "I'd swear that Wrendale didn't even know her! A damned impertinence, I call it.''

"Are you going to continue the hunt?" Marden asked. "After all, one battle does not make the war.''

Fortesque's defiance evaporated. "Not I," he said. "If Wrendale's after her, I haven't a chance.''

"Well, the Sutton gal ain't the only rich young woman in Town," Marden said practically. "What about the Buckham chit? She's said to be as rich as tolerably well-heeled.''

Fortesque shuddered. "She's as ugly as a pug dog! And only worse to come; if you want to know what she'll look like in thirty years, just look at her grandmama.'' He shuddered again.

"Well, I'm sure you'll come about," Marden said.

"Are you quite sure you couldn't see your way clear to...?" Fortesque began hopefully. Marden only stared at him; Fortesque wilted under his gaze. He rose and took up his hat and cane.

"Good morning, Willy," said Marden evenly. His friend nodded and made his way out.

Roger Marden turned and looked thoughtfully out the study window, watching Fortesque's disconsolate figure moving down the street. He was lucky, Marden reflected, that he had never yet come to the extremes Fortesque had. His "luck" at cards, Marden thought with a chuckle, combined with the liberal use of credit, had so far allowed him to afford the expensive trifles he found so necessary to a happy life. He looked round his study with a smile; though his home was small, every drapery and table, every individual appointment was of the finest quality.

Marden took a sip of brandy; his smile faded. London was becoming more and more expensive every day, unfortunately. Every day the cost of supporting his household rose, but Marden's winnings remained approximately the same. Already he had sensed one or two puzzled glances coming his way, as certain of his gentleman acquaintances wondered how his luck could be so consistently good. He dared not exercise his skill at clever cheating any more than he already did. Eventually, he realized, there might come a day when his winnings were insufficient to support his refined style of living.

Perhaps, Marden thought, perhaps he should think about finding a rich wife himself. Coldly, he weighed his assets. He was certainly eligible; though he had not inherited any great fortune, his birth was as good as any man's in England. He was generally held to be excessively handsome. And he did have a way with the ladies; charming the fairer sex had never presented any problem for Marden. He did not think he was flattering himself to believe that any woman on whom he turned his attention would be hard-pressed to resist. This Sutton girl, for instance, would no doubt be dazzled by the attentions of a handsome, worldly-wise man of gentle birth and excellent breeding. She might, Marden thought, be just what he needed.

Fortesque would be no hindrance; would Wrendale? If the earl were in fact attracted to the chit, he might prove to be a formidable enemy. Marden considered the matter. It was doubtful in the extreme, he decided, that a man so long unmarried and so patently not in need of a fortune as Wrendale would be seriously interested in marrying Margaret Sutton. It was more likely, Marden thought, that Fortesque had been making such an unbearable nuisance of himself that Wrendale had felt honour bound to do the gentlemanly thing and send Fortesque on his way. Still, just in the event there was a spark of interest there, it might be as well to keep an eye on Lord Wrendale, in addition to the myriad other suitors who were bound to pursue so rich a prize.

Marden twirled his brandy glass gently between his fingers. With the exercise of care and a modicum of wit, he thought, Margaret Sutton and all her lovely, lovely money would be his.

CHAPTER TWO

JOHNNY TREVORE TUGGED at his collar. "I don't know why you insisted on dragging me here, Wren," he grumbled. "It's the most insipid place in London. I've heard you say so dozens of times." He regarded Almack's Assembly Rooms with a jaundiced eye. Familiarly known as the "Marriage Mart," only the cream of the ton, and their sons and daughters, were able to acquire cards to attend the balls and assemblies held there. The Patronesses of Almack's, a group of well-born, well-connected ladies, ruled their domain with a fist of iron, rigidly defining what behaviour, and personages, were welcome at their august gatherings.

"Your mother would have my head if I didn't put you in the way of meeting eligible young ladies," Lord Wrendale said. "It also may help stop this talk that you're planning to marry Patsy Billington. It apparently has not occurred to you that if I have heard the gossip, then your mother has, too, or will soon."

"How could she, all the way in the country?" Johnny scoffed.

"There are always people," Wrendale said grimly, "absolutely burning to spread malicious gossip. You may be sure that someone will run to her with the story, sooner or later. Do you really wish for your mother to descend on London, full of ire and determined to save you from yourself?''

Johnny shuddered. ''Perish the thought!'' he said fervently. ''I love my mother, but . . .''

''But . . .!'' Wrendale agreed. They both laughed. ''I shall write to Lavinia this evening, assuring her that the rumours she may have heard have no basis in fact. If I also write that we have spent the evening at Almack's, and that you have met several eligible young ladies, I believe it shall go a long way towards soothing her fears.''

''She should know better than to believe gossip anyway,'' said Johnny. ''But just between us, Wren, I have absolutely no intention of marrying anyone. I'm far too happy being footloose and unattached to willingly leg-shackle myself.''

''You have responsibilities,'' Wrendale said, raising his quizzing glass to scan the room. ''Don't forget what you owe to your name and your family.''

Johnny hooted, causing one stuffy-looking gentleman in knee breeches to turn towards them, frowning. Lord Wrendale fixed his quizzing glass on the man; the curious gentleman quickly found something else to occupy his attention.

''Do try to control your outbursts, John,'' Wrendale said. ''We may know you to be a half-witted young fool, but we don't want the whole world to know it, do we?''

''Yes, but really, Wren,'' Johnny said. ''You, spouting off to me about what I owe my family? I shouldn't owe them anything at all if I weren't your heir, and I wouldn't be your heir if you would marry.''

Wrendale shrugged. ''Every family,'' he said, ''is allowed one eccentric bachelor. In this family, I am that eccentric. It may seem selfish of me, but there! The old are ever willing to sacrifice the young.''

"Well, you can't make me marry," Johnny said. "And you wouldn't even if you could; despite your talk, Wren, I know you too well to believe that you'd ever be so tyrannical.''

"Regrettably, you are correct," Lord Wrendale said. "I would never compel you to marry." He turned to his nephew, eyes alight with laughter. "But your mother, Johnny, your mother most assuredly would!''

Across the room, Lady Sally Carstairs observed the arrival of Wrendale and young Johnny Trevore. "Come along, Meg," she said. She grasped Meg firmly by the wrist.

Meg perceived the direction of her preceptress's gaze. "Oh, no," she said firmly. "I'll not pursue an acquaintance with such an overbearing prig as Wrendale, Aunt Sally.''

"You will find, my dear," Lady Carstairs said, "that it is 'prigs' like Wrendale that can make or break a young lady's chances in Town. He is a social arbiter; it would be terribly foolish for you to court his displeasure.''

"I'll take my chances, thank you," Meg said.

"But you promised, Meg," Sally Carstairs said reproachfully.

Meg heaved an exasperated sigh. "Very well, Aunt.''

Lady Carstairs sailed across the crowded room, Meg in tow.

"Good evening, Wrendale," she said. "I believe that you have not been presented to my charge, Miss Margaret Sutton. Meg, my dear, this is Lord Wrendale.''

Meg felt as though the smile were plastered to her face; the glint in Wrendale's blue eyes made her grit her teeth. "Good evening, my lord."

Wrendale bowed over her hand. "Charmed," he said. "Though I believe that Miss Sutton and I may have met before?" His smile made Meg long to slap him. "Under somewhat singular circumstances, as I recall." He turned to his nephew. "May I present my nephew, John Trevore?"

Meg turned on John such a brilliant smile that it made him blink. "How very nice to meet you, Mr. Trevore," she said.

"Charmed," he said, looking back and forth between his uncle and Meg.

"Why don't you children go off and dance?" Sally Carstairs said. "As Meg has already received permission from the Patronesses to waltz, it would be a shame for her to sit out the dance. Don't you agree, Mr. Trevore?"

John rose to the occasion. "It would be my pleasure. Miss Sutton?" He held out his arm and, after a moment's hesitation, Meg took it.

"A trifle ham-handed, wouldn't you say, Sally?" Wrendale remarked, watching Meg and Johnny whirl away.

"Perhaps, but I did wish to speak to you," Sally Carstairs said. "I understand that I owe you my thanks for saving Meg from a difficult situation."

Wrendale shrugged. "It was nothing, I assure you. And I doubt that Miss Sutton would join you in thanking me."

"No, she wouldn't," Lady Carstairs said bluntly. "But I don't want you to get the wrong idea about her.

Meg's a good girl, Wrendale. A trifle inexperienced, mayhap, but good.''

"I have no doubt," Wrendale said.

"And I hope…that is to say, I know that you won't bruit about her little error in judgement?''

Wrendale turned to Lady Carstairs and raised his quizzing glass. "Are you suggesting," he asked coldly, "that I might spread gossip about Miss Sutton?''

"Of course not," Sally said soothingly. "'Tis just…oh, Wrendale, I am so woefully green at this chaperon business!" she confessed. "I should hate to see the girl ruin her Season before it's even begun.''

Wrendale softened. "Think no more about it," he said with a smile. "The matter is quite forgotten. And I daresay it won't happen again; I read the child quite a scold before I was done with her." He chuckled. "Miss Sutton may never forgive me my impertinence, but I don't think she'll ever forget it, either.''

"Exactly my point," Lady Carstairs exclaimed. "She was angry with you, I'll not deny it, but you made quite an impression on her. We've known each other a long time, Wrendale, and though we've never been what you would call bosom bows, I was wondering…could you see your way clear to lending me a hand with the girl?''

"I beg your pardon?''

"If you could just keep an eye out for her," Lady Carstairs said. "You know—steer her away from bad company, give her the hint if any of the gentlemen she knows are not *comme il faut*." She stared up at Wrendale entreatingly. "It would be such a help to me!''

Wrendale shook his head firmly. "No, thank you," he said. "The role of wet nurse is a little outside my experience."

"But—"

Wrendale held a finger up to Lady Sally Carstairs's lips. "Pray do not compel me to give you one of my famous set-downs," he said. "I wish that I might oblige you, Sally, but the answer is no."

On the dance floor, Meg burned with embarrassment. "I'm so sorry," she said.

Johnny looked surprised. "For what?" he asked.

"The way Aunt Sally forced you to dance with me," Meg said miserably.

"I never need to be forced to dance with a beautiful young lady," Johnny said gallantly.

"Yes, but she was so very transparent," Meg blurted out. "Such blatant matchmaking quite mortifies me."

"I don't think that was it at all," Johnny said. "Look; she and my uncle have their heads together. They probably just wished to have a comfortable cose."

"Oh, no," Meg said grimly. "Aunt Sally is quite determined to marry me off. Hunchbacked, squint-eyed or lame, she'll find me a husband."

Johnny roared with laughter. "Surely I'm not as bad as all that?" he teased. Meg started to stammer an apology; Johnny shook his head firmly. "Don't apologize," he said. "Those are the first honest words I've ever heard at Almack's, or anywhere else among the ton, for that matter. I like you, Miss Margaret Sutton."

Meg smiled shyly. "I like you, too," she said.

"Shall we be friends, then?" Johnny said. "Mind you, I've no desire to dangle after you; marriage is not a state to which I aspire."

It was Meg's turn to blink. "I feel the same way myself," she confessed.

"A kindred spirit!" Johnny cried. "I must allow, I never thought to meet a young lady as disinterested in stepping into parson's mousetrap as I am myself. Let us start a club, shall we? We two shall be the only members, and we'll call it . . ."

"The Freedom Club!" Meg giggled, amused by Johnny's nonsense and his twinkling blue eyes.

"Are we agreed, then? We two and no more? And absolute honesty between us at all times," Johnny said. The music came to an end.

"Done!" Meg answered. The two solemnly shook hands, ignoring the curious stares of the other dancers.

"Pardon me." Meg and Johnny turned to find Willy Fortesque at Johnny's elbow. Meg stiffened.

"Trevore, old boy, I wonder if you'll allow me to spirit Miss Sutton away for a moment."

Johnny frowned. "I really don't think . . ." he began.

"Should let the lady decide, don't you think?" Fortesque said. He turned to Meg. "I won't take more than a minute of your time, Miss Sutton," he said.

Meg hesitated, then shrugged. "Very well." She smiled at Johnny. "It's all right, Mr. Trevore," she said. "Truly."

Johnny's frown did not lessen; he knew of Fortesque, and of the man's unsavoury reputation. "If that is what you wish," he said disapprovingly. He bowed. Meg watched him walk away, then turned back to Fortesque.

"What is it you want, Mr. Fortesque?" she asked in a chilly tone. "After our last meeting, quite frankly I have nothing to say to you."

"But it is our last meeting that I wish to discuss," Willy Fortesque said, with what he imagined to be an ingratiating smile. He put a hand under her elbow and guided her behind a group of potted palms which hid them from most of the other guests.

Meg pulled her arm free. "I have no wish to be private with you, sir."

The man held up a hand. "I only want to offer you a sincere apology, Miss Sutton," he said. "My behaviour the other evening was inexcusable."

"It was," Meg agreed.

"I can only plead the twin exigencies of moonlight and your own great beauty," he said. "I quite lost my head."

"One can only hope," Meg said drily, "that the moon does not always affect you so. Else you would be advised to be abroad only during the daylight hours."

Fortesque laughed heartily. "Indeed, you may be right," he said. "Do say that you forgive me, Miss Sutton," he added earnestly. "I behaved very badly, I know, but can you be hard-hearted enough to hold it against me forever?" After thinking the matter over, Willy Fortesque had convinced himself that he still had a chance with Margaret Sutton, so long as he could catch her when Lord Wrendale was not at hand. Thus, he had made sure that Wrendale was safely engaged elsewhere before approaching Meg.

"As far as I am concerned, Mr. Fortesque, the matter is closed," Meg said. She met his gaze squarely. "But understand, if you will, that I have no desire to entertain your suit. I will turn you down firmly if you are ever unwise enough to press the matter."

Fortesque looked crestfallen. "But Miss Sutton, you are being most unjust," he whined. "I did apologize manfully; you should, in all fairness, give me the opportunity to make it up to you."

"If you'll excuse me, Mr. Fortesque..." Meg said disdainfully. She started to turn away.

Willy Fortesque reached out to grab her wrist. "I say, don't be so top-lofty!" he cried. "I only want to—"

A handsome blond gentleman moved round the pillar and clamped a hand on Fortesque's shoulder. "That's quite enough, Willy," he said. "Let her go."

Fortesque jumped. "Marden!" he said. "There's no need for you to interfere. This is a private conversation."

"I don't believe the lady agrees with you," Marden said. "In point of fact, she appears," he added as he smiled at Meg, "to be positively longing for interference."

"But I—" Fortesque began.

"Don't be tiresome, Willy," Marden said. "Take yourself off." He pointedly turned away from his friend and smiled again at Meg.

Fortesque hesitated for a moment, then, with a long face and dragging steps, obeyed Marden and departed.

Meg reached out impulsively and squeezed Marden's hand. "Thank you," she said. "I'm sorry to say this if Mr. Fortesque is a friend of yours, but he is the most awful mushroom!''

Marden laughed. "He is indeed," he agreed. "I often wonder why I bother with him; it must be because our mothers were dear friends. The burdens of family can be heavy at times." Meg agreed with a smile. "But we have not been introduced," he said. "Mr. Roger Marden, at your service, ma'am."

"I am Margaret Sutton," Meg said. "And you have already been of the greatest possible service to me."

"Then might I presume on that service and call upon you tomorrow?" Marden asked. He smiled sheepishly. "In truth, I am much better able to understand Fortesque's ardour now that I've had a good look at you!"

Since they were at Almack's, Meg thought, the man must be respectable. And Aunt Sally did want her to meet eligible gentlemen. "Of course you may," she said. "I really am most awfully grateful, you know."

Marden held out his arm. "May I escort you back to your mother, Miss Sutton?"

Meg took his arm. "My aunt, actually," she said. "Or rather, an aunt by courtesy—she was my mama's closest friend."

"Ah, another of those family burdens," Marden said with a smile.

"Not in this case," Meg replied. "Aunt Sally is the dearest, sweetest thing in nature."

As they stepped out from behind the greenery, Johnny Trevore came hurrying up. "Miss Sutton!" he said. "Lord, I've been looking everywhere for you." He nodded at Marden. "Marden," he said coolly.

Roger Marden released Meg's arm. "I see you have yet another swain, Miss Sutton," he said cheerfully.

"I'll leave you to him." He bent over her hand. "Until tomorrow?"

"Tomorrow," Meg agreed.

Johnny waited until Marden was out of earshot. "Miss Sutton..." he began.

"Do call me Meg, won't you?" Meg said. "And I shall call you Johnny. After all, we are members of the same club, are we not?"

"That is why I am presuming to speak to you on a subject that is really no concern of mine," Johnny said. "I..." He looked about, then said, "Oh, do come back here, where we may speak in private for a moment." He pulled her behind the same potted palms which Fortesque had chosen. "Meg, you need to be more careful about whom you befriend," he said. "Fortesque, for example; a more thorough bounder never lived."

"As well I know!" Meg said fervently. "You needn't worry about him, Johnny. I daresay I've seen the last of Mr. Fortesque."

"And Marden," Johnny continued. "Something not quite right about him, either."

"Oh, but Johnny, he was so very kind," Meg said. "He positively rescued me from Fortesque. I am really most grateful to him."

"And what have we here?" came a silky voice. "Johnny, you scamp!"

Johnny Trevore turned, and Meg saw a horrified expression flash across his face. "Mama!" he cried.

"Gracious, Johnny, anyone would think that you weren't pleased to see me," Lavinia Trevore said. She was magnificent in purple satin, a plume of matching feathers in her hair. "Come and kiss me, dearest."

Johnny planted a tentative kiss on his mother's powdered cheek. "'Twas just that you startled me, Mama," he said. He turned to Meg. "Me... Miss Sutton, may I present my mother, Mrs. Lavinia Trevore? Mama, this is Miss Margaret Sutton, a friend of mine."

Meg curtsied. "How do you do, ma'am," she murmured.

Lavinia took her hand. "But how charming!" she said with a smile. Meg could not help but notice that despite the lady's kind words, her eyes were positively boring into her. "Tell me, Miss Sutton, do you reside in Town?" Lavinia continued. "I don't believe I've heard the name..."

"I am staying with Lady Sally Carstairs," Meg said. "Perhaps you knew my father—Thomas Sutton?"

"Miser Sutton?" Lavinia breathed; her eyes widened. "My Lord!" she said faintly.

Johnny squirmed with embarrassment. "I'm quite sure that Miss Sutton will excuse us, Mama," he said, "so that we might have a private moment. Won't you, Miss Sutton?"

"Pray don't be absurd, Johnny," Lavinia said, tucking Meg's arm into her own. She began to lead Meg inexorably across the hall, her son following behind. "There is nothing I should like better than to become better acquainted with this delightful young lady."

"Mama, please!" Johnny hissed.

"Do hush," Lavinia said. She turned her attention to Meg. "Tell me, my dear, is this your first visit to London?"

"It is," Meg said. "My father was not overly fond of city life."

"Indeed, I agree with him," Lavinia said. "I seldom venture to visit Town myself. But as I had not seen Johnny in some time, I decided to come and surprise him. You were surprised, weren't you, my pet?"

"Completely," Johnny said, with an irony which was lost on his mother.

"But I fear that I chose a poor moment for my appearance," Lavinia said with a chuckle. "You children were smelling of April and May, back behind your palms. 'Twas very naughty of you to sneak off, but ah, well! Young love will triumph, will it not?"

"Mama!" Johnny cried. Meg could only blush in confusion.

Across the room, Lord Wrendale watched them. He had seen Lavinia Trevore enter Almack's some time ago and observed, with some amusement, her frenzied search for her son. Wrendale assumed that Lavinia had gone to his home and learned from Stubbs where he and Johnny were to be found this evening. Lavinia had then apparently wasted no time in changing her clothing and rushing off to join them. He chuckled as he saw his sister-in-law's brilliant smile; there was no doubt that Johnny had introduced her to Margaret Sutton, and that Lavinia knew of the girl's immense fortune. Meg's blush and Johnny's outraged expression, however, made Wrendale judge it time to intervene. He crossed to join them.

"Lavinia," he said, bowing over her hand. "What an unexpected pleasure."

"Wrendale." Lavinia nodded. "I presume that you have met Miss Sutton?"

"I have," Wrendale said. "As a matter of fact, she promised me this dance. Miss Sutton?" He held out his arm.

Meg hesitated for a moment, torn between her dislike of the earl and her desire to escape from Lavinia Trevore's heavy-handed jocularity. "Thank you, my lord," she said finally. She took his arm.

"But, Wrendale," Lavinia said with a rigid smile, "wouldn't you prefer to let Johnny take your dance, so that you and I might visit together?"

"As you will no doubt be staying in my home, Lavinia, I'm sure that we'll have quite enough time to visit," Wrendale said pleasantly. "Your servant." He bowed and led Meg away, onto the dance floor.

"Well, have I earned a little forgiveness, Miss Sutton?" Wrendale asked.

"I beg your pardon?"

"For rescuing you from my redoubtable sister-in-law," he said. "Surely that must have made your heart soften at least a little bit towards me."

"Mrs. Trevore was most charming," Meg said stiffly.

"I'm sure she was," Wrendale said. "Crushingly gracious and not overly subtle, I'd guess, but excessively charming, without a doubt."

Meg swallowed a little choke of laughter. "You are quite the rudest man I've ever met," she said.

"Too true, I fear," Wrendale acknowledged. "I am renowned for it, in fact."

"'Tis not a quality which I should wish to be known for," Meg said honestly.

"Yes, but you are a beautiful young woman," he pointed out. "I, on the other hand, am a hardened old curmudgeon. The cases are very different."

"You're not so old as all that," Meg said, in what she considered to be a dispassionate tone.

"A compliment, my dear? You quite unman me," Wrendale said.

Meg was suddenly very conscious of the strength of Wrendale's arm curved about her, and the warmth of his hand pressed against the small of her back. For a fleeting moment she wondered what Lord Wrendale was really like; surely that cool facade which he presented to the world could not be all there was to the gentleman.

They danced without speaking for a few moments. Wrendale looked down at Meg and thought again how lovely she was. A pity that the child should be so headstrong, and so very loath to admit her inexperience. Wrendale felt a pang of pity for Sally Carstairs, so determined yet so manifestly unequipped to oversee the schooling of such a filly. Perhaps he should reconsider and lend Sally a hand, he thought; it would not be so very much trouble, after all.

"You seem quite taken with my nephew, Miss Sutton," Wrendale said.

"I find Mr. Trevore most delightful," Meg answered. "Though not very like you, I'm afraid."

Wrendale laughed. "A hit!" he said. "I am suitably repaid for daring to think that you complimented me." His reward was a brief smile from Meg. "Yes," he continued, "Johnny is a good lad. But not, alas, a promising prospect as a husband."

Meg stiffened in his arms. "That is no concern of mine," she said.

"I'm glad to hear you say that," Wrendale said. "I feared that you might regard Johnny in a romantic light; 'twould not be wise, my dear. I don't believe that you two should suit."

"Your beliefs are of no moment, my lord, as Johnny and I are nothing but friends," Meg said icily.

"Good," Wrendale said. "Johnny is yet too young to choose a life's mate." He smiled down at Meg. "For instance, looking at you, poor Johnny would see only your beauty, and ignore the temper indicated by that pugnacious little chin." He lightly touched the afore-mentioned feature. "Johnny could never be happy with a woman with such strength of character; he's far too easily swayed by feminine wiles for that."

"That is Johnny's affair, don't you think?" Meg said angrily. "Or do you feel that you have as much right to interfere in Johnny's life as you apparently do in everyone else's?"

"A man has a right to have an eye to his nephew's well-being," Wrendale said. "And if I have inter-fered, as you put it, in your life, you should be glad of it. Need I remind you that I saved you from God knows what at the hands of Mr. Fortesque?"

Meg could feel colour rising into her cheeks. "I was perfectly able to manage Mr. Fortesque myself," she said. "There was no need for you to rescue me."

Wrendale laughed. "You'll forgive me if I say that it did not appear so at the time; you looked for all the world like a foolish child, in over her head and about to drown."

"And you will forgive me," Meg snapped, "if I tell you that you are the most ill-mannered, insuffer-able...!" She stopped, and took a deep breath. "I'll not stay and be insulted by you any further, my lord." Meg wrenched herself out of his arms and turned to stride off the floor, leaving Lord Wrendale standing alone in the midst of the dancers.

CHAPTER THREE

PATSY BILLINGTON FROWNED at her reflection in the mirror. Was that a line? She groped among the score of bottles and jars which littered her dressing-table and, choosing one, smoothed the scented lotion it contained onto the offending patch of skin. It couldn't be, she told herself firmly; why, just last night young Johnny Trevore had praised her skin, telling her in his boyish way that it was like a perfect peach, all smooth and rosy. Bless that Johnny! What a sweet lad he was, and so very generous, too. Not at all like some she'd known in her time; no, not at all.

Patsy Billington had started her life in a tenant's cottage in Scotland. She had been a very pretty child and had grown into a beautiful young woman. The landowner's eldest son had discovered her when she was seventeen. In addition to making her his mistress, it had amused him to teach her the ways of a lady—the proper way to walk and talk, how to entertain and be entertained and the way in which a true-born lady dressed and comported herself. He had done his work too well for his own liking, much to his chagrin. Patsy had met one of his friends, a Mr. Billington, and the friend, quite besotted by Patsy's beauty, had offered Patsy marriage.

Newly married, Patsy had come to London with her husband. She was thrilled to discover that he moved among the ton, albeit on the fringes, and that she, by virtue of being his wife, was also allowed an entrée into that heady world. Though she had never attained vouchers to Almack's or been invited to the very best parties, Patsy still was able to move among the well-born and well-heeled, and for a time, it had seemed as though life were perfect.

Then her husband died, quite suddenly, and Patsy had found herself to be penniless. Mr. Billington's unfortunate addiction to gaming had cost him everything he had. Faced with the prospect of returning to her parents' cottage in Scotland, a prospect which filled the lively young woman with horror, she had taken the only alternative which had presented itself.

Patsy sighed. It had been many years, and several lovers, since she had decided that anything was better than returning to the boredom and poverty of Scotland. And it had not worked out too badly, taken all in all, she told herself. She might be notorious, but she had managed to retain her position on the fringes of the ton and to acquire certain assets that soon, very soon would allow her to put into motion her plan.

With an impatient movement, Patsy pushed herself away from the dressing-table. Calling to her maid, she quickly arrayed herself in a demure gown of grey silk, chuckling to herself to think what her friends would say to see her in so drab a garment.

"Miss Patsy," her maid said, "the young gentleman is here to see you. Shall I show him up?"

"No!" Patsy said. "Tell him . . . tell him that I have the headache, and that I wish to rest quietly today. Then wait until he leaves and send for my carriage."

The maid curtsied and left the room, and Patsy sat down to wait. If all went well, she thought with a shiver of excitement, tonight might see the end of her notorious career. She hoped that Johnny would not be too upset; she would hate to hurt him. But it was for the best, really. It was time that he turned his thoughts to meeting a young lady whom he might marry. She should not have let him become her protector in the first place, she knew. Johnny Trevore was too young for a lady of her experience, and her conscience had troubled her over taking his money. But he had been so eager, and so very charming...!

Her maid returned. Patsy threw a cloak over her dress, pulling the hood up to hide her face, and made her way down to the carriage.

Patsy's destination was across Town, in a part of the City devoted to banks and financial institutions. The plaque on the wall of the small brick building she entered read Brown and Brown; only those of some financial acumen would have recognized the name of the firm, known as much for its honesty as its shrewd judgement.

"Mrs. Billington!" The elderly man bowed her into his office. "How delightful it is to see you. May I offer you some tea?"

Patsy shook her head. "If you don't mind, Mr. Brown, I have another appointment soon. Shall we get right down to business?" Patsy opened her reticule and handed the man a thick roll of banknotes.

"Very good, Mrs. Billington," Mr. Brown said. "But you didn't need to come all the way here just to make a deposit. I could have sent a messenger to you."

"I didn't," Patsy said bluntly. "I wished to check on the status of my investments."

Mr. Brown hemmed and hawed. He pulled a thick, dusty ledger towards himself. "Let me just refresh my

memory, Mrs. Billington," he said. He opened the
book and ran a gnarled finger over the pages, grunt-
ing to himself every so often.

"Well?" Patsy asked sharply. "Have I enough
money?"

"Hmm, hmm," Mr. Brown murmured. "'Enough
money' is a somewhat imprecise term, my dear lady."

Patsy stifled an impatient sigh. "Enough money to
buy a small piece of property in London and to live
quietly," she said. "Enough to afford not the extrav-
agancies of life, but its elegancies. Enough money to
live without having to economize or worry."

"I should say... not, I'm afraid, Mrs. Billington,"
Mr. Brown said. "You are close, very close indeed, but
not quite there yet, I think." He regarded his client
sympathetically.

Patsy's shoulders slumped. "But I thought...I was
sure...!"

"Let me explain," said Mr. Brown, not unkindly.
"Many of your investments have done well, very well,
but one or two have proved to be somewhat of a disappointment. I did warn you when you first came to
me, many years ago, that I could not make you promises."

"Of course you did," Patsy said, pulling herself
together. "And I could not have chosen anyone who
would look after my funds more diligently or honestly than you have, Mr. Brown." She straightened her
shoulders. "How much more do I require?"

Mr. Brown hemmed and hawed again. "You understand that there is no set figure?" he said. "I have
tried to calculate carefully, allowing for the constant
rise in the cost of maintaining an establishment and
figuring in a cushion for any unexpected expenses."

Patsy nodded. "Then I should say—" the elderly man cleared his throat "—that another five thousand pounds should assure you of a lifetime of comfort."

"Five thousand pounds!" Patsy whispered.

Mr. Brown looked troubled. "Perhaps I have been too conservative," he said. "It may well be that you have enough now." He smiled a bleak smile. "I am an old man, Mrs. Billington, and hence, somewhat gloomy in my outlook."

"No," Patsy said with decision. "I trust your judgement. If you say five thousand pounds, then five thousand pounds it is. I'll raise it." She rose to her feet and held out her hand. "Thank you, Mr. Brown," she said. "I won't take up any more of your time."

Mr. Brown watched the woman leave his office and shook his head. However she came by the money she invested with him, he could not help but admire the beautiful Mrs. Billington and her determination to make a new life for herself. He sincerely hoped that she would raise that last bit of money, and achieve the goal which she had worked towards for so long.

"HOW COULD YOU ALLOW this to happen, Wrendale?" Lavinia Trevore scolded. "I think it too, too bad of you."

Lord Wrendale sighed. "Lavinia," he said, "I assure you, you're becoming upset over nothing at all."

"Nothing?" she sniffed. "You may call the future happiness of my only child nothing, but I do not."

In an attempt to distract her, Wrendale said, "How ever did you hear of it in the first place?"

"That odious Milland woman, of course." Lavinia sniffed again. "If you could have seen her, Wrendale, so solicitous, acting as though she wasn't positively relishing bringing me such news. She's always been jealous of me, of course, because of her husband.''

"Lavinia!" teased Wrendale.

"Well, with her face and figure it was no wonder her husband made calf eyes at me. It would have made you laugh to see the way that large, lumpish man used to clump along after me, for all the world like a great puppy, with Lady Milland always hard on his heels, watching to make sure that nothing illicit happened. As if I would have anything to do with such an oaf, when I had your own dear brother to love." Lavinia dabbed at her eyes with a scrap of lace-edged hand-kerchief. "How I do miss him!"

"Lord Milland?" Wrendale asked with a wicked smile.

"Of course not!" Lavinia gasped, then, catching sight of her brother-in-law's face, shook a finger at him. "Yes, you will have your little jokes, won't you?" she said bitterly. "But that shan't save my Johnny from the clutches of the Billington woman."

"I promise you, Lavinia, he isn't in anyone's clutches," Wrendale said. "He's just a young man, behaving in a way that young men have since the dawn of time."

"You gentlemen always stick together, don't you?" Lavinia said. "In the face of feminine disapproval, the worst of enemies will join forces as though they were brothers."

"Johnny and I are not enemies, and there is really nothing for you to worry about," Wrendale said. "We have discussed the matter and—"

"Do you mean to say," Lavinia said slowly, "that you have encouraged Johnny in his pursuit of that . . . that harlot? How could you, Wrendale? How could you be so wicked?''

"As a matter of fact, I advised him to make an end to it," Wrendale said calmly. "Sadly, he was not inclined to take my advice, but he has no intention of behaving foolishly, of that I am quite sure." He leaned forward, his hands clasped loosely before him. "If you were wise, Lavinia, you'd go home. There truly is no cause for concern."

"No." Lavinia's mouth set mulishly. "I shan't go home until Johnny is safely wed."

"Marriage?" Wrendale quirked an eyebrow. "He's a tad young for that, isn't he?"

"I might have agreed with you six months ago, but the situation has changed," Lavinia said. "A wife is precisely what John needs."

"And have you yet chosen the unfortunate young woman that is to be his bride?" Wrendale asked drily.

"Why, Miss Sutton, of course," Lavinia said, as though it were the most obvious thing in the world.

"Of course," Wrendale said. "I might have known!"

"Mind you, after her actions last night at Almack's, I did have some second thoughts," Lavinia said. "Speaking of Almack's, Wrendale, I take it very ill that you insisted on dancing with Miss Sutton, when Johnny might have taken the opportunity to pursue his acquaintance with her," Lavinia continued. "I won't say that you were well served for your insensitivity, but . . ." She shrugged.

"I see—the entire incident was my fault, was it?"

"Well, I won't go so far as that," Lavinia admitted. "What did you say to her?"

"I foolishly ventured to offer the chit advice," he growled. "Regarding a matter of the heart."

Lavinia leaned forward eagerly. "Do tell," she breathed. "Did Johnny's name come up? Did she mention him?"

"She did," Wrendale said reluctantly. "But you mustn't think—"

"Wonderful!" Lavinia clapped her hands. "'Twas good of you, Wrendale, to have an eye to Johnny's interests. Well? Did she seem taken with him?"

"She said she liked him, but it wasn't—"

"Miss Sutton must be interested in Johnny, if she discussed him with you," Lavinia said with great satisfaction. "She'll do very nicely, I think. I don't say that it wasn't very naughty of her to behave as she did with you, but I have no doubt 'twas merely a case of an overindulged child who has not been taught the proper way to go along. After all, what else can one expect, with that fool Sally Carstairs for a guardian?"

"Miss Sutton's fortune does excuse a multitude of sins, doesn't it?" Wrendale said sarcastically.

"One must be practical, Wrendale," Lavinia said uneasily. "She is the catch of the Season; one may forgive her a great deal on that score."

"Ah, Mammon!" Wrendale murmured.

"Yes, it's all very well for you to take that high and mighty attitude," Lavinia said irritably. "But I've a son to think of, and I believe that Miss Sutton would make him a very good wife."

"Have you yet told Johnny about your plans for him?" Wrendale asked.

"No, but I shall," Lavinia said. "There's not a moment to lose; I should like to see Johnny married before Christmas."

"Are you aware that Johnny has absolutely no desire to wed?" Wrendale asked. "Does that matter at all?"

"My Johnny is a good boy," Lavinia said stubbornly. "He will trust that I know what's best for him, I have no doubt."

"He may prove to be less biddable than you think, Lavinia," Wrendale said. "In fact, I should be quite amazed if he did not."

Lavinia allowed herself a smug smile. "You may find him to be intractable," she said, "but there is very little that a young man will not do to please his mama."

"You are wasting your time, Lavinia," Wrendale said. "And doing him a great disservice, I might add. Johnny is not ready to stand husband to any lady, much less a headstrong hoyden four years his senior!"

"You are, of course, entitled to your opinion," Lavinia Trevore said. "But I am quite, quite determined. Johnny shall be betrothed this Season, and to Miss Margaret Sutton."

MEG SUTTON LOOKED both ways, then slipped across the hall into the drawing-room. She shut the double doors behind her and leaned back against them with a sigh. Thank goodness she had finally managed to elude Aunt Sally!

Lady Sally Carstairs had been furious with Meg for leaving Wrendale alone on the dance floor at Almack's. All the way home, the previous night, Sally had read her a thundering scold. Sally had never allowed Meg to explain her actions; in Sally's words, there was "simply no excuse for such rudeness!"

This morning at breakfast, and again over luncheon, Sally had resumed her remonstrances as though the conversation had never been interrupted.

"You've quite ruined your chances in London, Meg," Sally had said. "It might be best if I were to send you back to the country."

"Surely not?" Meg had answered, aghast. "Do you not think that you may be exaggerating the importance of last night's...incident?"

Sally had laughed bitterly. "I wish that I might think so," she had said. "But you insulted one of England's best-born peers, and did it in front of the entire ton, near enough. I don't think I could exaggerate the damage that this has done to your reputation. They will call you fast, and say that you know no better than to tie your garter in public."

"Well, I shan't go home," Meg had said firmly. "I am my own mistress now. You have been kind enough to introduce me to Society, Aunt Sally, and for that, I am most grateful. But you are not my guardian. I am in charge of my own future." She laughed bitterly. "My father's death set me free. I can't think why he didn't appoint a trustee to oversee my fortune, but he didn't."

"I think that he didn't expect to die when you were still so young, relatively speaking," Sally had said, distracted. "I think that he envisioned you a woman in her thirties or forties, well able to look after a fortune on her own."

"Well, for whatever reason, I am free," Meg had said. "From this point on, I shall make my own decisions about where I go and what I do."

Her words to Sally had been brave, but now, alone with her thoughts, Meg sighed again. She crossed the room to sink into a chair before the fireplace. What was the point? she asked herself. If Aunt Sally were right, and the ton did turn the shoulder on her, there would be no sense in staying in London. Perhaps she would travel, she thought, brightening a little; the one consolation of great wealth was that it would enable her to do as she pleased.

Stubbs, Lady Carstairs's butler, entered the room and cleared his throat. "A caller for you, Miss Margaret," he said. "A Mr. Marden."

"Oh, Stubbs, I don't think—" Meg began.

"Too late, I fear," came a cheery voice. Roger Marden entered the room behind Stubbs. "So willing was I to impose on your gratitude that I followed your butler in," he said. "Don't blame him, poor fellow; I don't think he even knew that I was behind him." Marden crossed the room to bow over Meg's hand. "I needn't ask how you find yourself; your radiance shames the sun." These words were spoken with such a droll expression that Meg could not help but laugh.

"Good morning to you, Mr. Marden," she said. "Stubbs, would you be a dear and fetch us some tea? Or would you prefer something stronger, Mr. Marden?"

"Thank you, nothing for me," Marden said.

Stubbs bowed and left the drawing-room, leaving the door carefully ajar behind him.

Marden sat down near Meg. "How are you, really?" he asked gently.

Meg tried to be lighthearted. "What, has the sun outshone me so soon?"

Marden smiled apologetically at her. "I know that we aren't very well acquainted," he said, "and that I am the most forward of dogs to speak to you so. But really, you should not take it too much to heart."

Meg tried to smile back at him but failed miserably. "You saw, then."

"I did," Marden replied. "I daresay Lady Carstairs has been predicting doom for you all this day?"

"Indeed she has!" Meg laughed unsteadily.

"I shouldn't place too much stock in her gloomy prognostications, if I were you. Lady Carstairs is an estimable woman, but, like many of her generation, she is too easily shocked, I have no doubt." Roger Marden shrugged delicately. "She thinks of the way things were when she was a girl, and forgets that the world has changed. Twenty years ago, it would have been your ruin, but today? I think not, particularly as your partner, or victim," he grinned suddenly, "was Wrendale."

"What has that to say to the matter?" Meg asked, beginning to feel a little bit more cheerful.

"My lord Wrendale, 'the Cynic,' as he is called, has offended more people in London than any six other peers put together," Marden said. "Many of us have been the butt of my lord's famed wit; I'd wager my last shilling that I was not the only person at Almack's last night that silently cheered when you put him in his place." Marden leaned forward in his chair, his expression serious. "Your friends, if I may call myself one, know that Wrendale must have offered you some provocation too great to be borne."

"He did, as it happens," Meg said. "Not that any-one will be interested in that, according to my aunt."

"That is where she and I must part company," Marden said. "I believe that Wrendale's known rude-ness will make the ton realize that the fault was his, not yours."

"How I hope that you may prove to be correct," Meg said. "I don't think that..."

Lady Sally Carstairs swept into the drawing-room, her attempt at frigid regality somewhat impaired by the fact that her chignon had slipped and come to rest over her left ear. "Meg, you naughty creature," she said, her colour high. "To entertain a gentleman alone! What will Mr. Marden think of us?"

"Why, that you are charming, of course," Marden said, bowing over Sally's hand. "As is your proté-gée." He helped the older woman to a chair. "I was just telling Miss Sutton how very glad we are that you have invited her to stay. I was about to try to convince her to allow me to show her some of our good Town when you came in; won't you help me?"

"I should love to go," Meg said. She added hastily, "if that meets with your approval, Aunt Sally?"

"We shall see," Sally said grimly. "I am not con-vinced that a pleasure jaunt would be in Meg's best interest at this time."

"I must warn you, then—I shall try to change your mind!" Marden said.

Stubbs re-entered the drawing-room. "John Tre-vore to see Miss Margaret, my lady," he said.

Lady Carstairs's expression lightened. "Do show him in, Stubbs," she said.

Johnny Trevore entered the room, looking for all the world as though he were going to the block. His body drooped, and all the sparkle had gone out of his blue eyes. "Good day, Lady Carstairs," he said. "Good day, Me...Miss Sutton." He nodded curtly. "Marden."

"'Twas good of you to call, Johnny," Sally Carstairs said with a warm smile. "Won't you come here and sit by me?" She patted the seat beside her.

"Ah...certainly," Johnny said. He shot an entreating look at Meg, then settled down beside Lady Carstairs.

"How is your dear mama, Johnny? I understand that she has come to Town. I'm sure that we are most pleased to have her back in our midst. Does she plan a long stay?"

"I believe that her plans are uncertain at this time," Johnny said. He stared across the room with a look which seemed to Meg to be fraught with meaning; she could only frown back, puzzled.

Stubbs returned to the drawing-room, his normal impassive countenance pulled down into a frown. He hurried to Lady Carstairs and, leaning over, murmured something in her ear.

"Devil take that man!" Sally exclaimed. "I vow, 'tis the last time I shall have a French chef, however well they may cook." She rose. "I must go down to the kitchens, Meg," she said. "Monsoor Henri is pitching a fit over some bad fish." She cast an uncertain look at Meg's two callers, then, making up her mind, she said, "I'll return in a moment. You gentlemen may bear Meg company while I am gone." She bustled out of the drawing-room, Stubbs at her heels.

"Thank God!" Johnny said. "I must speak to you, Meg." He shot a look at Marden. "It's urgent."

Roger Marden rose gracefully to his feet. "I shan't tarry, then," he said. He bowed over Meg's hand. "*Au revoir,* Miss Sutton." He turned to Johnny. "Good day, Trevore." His expression was unreadable.

Johnny waited until Marden's footsteps had faded away into silence before crossing the room to drop down beside Meg. "Lord, Meg," he said miserably, "I am in such a muddle!"

"What is it, Johnny?"

"It's my mother," Johnny confessed. "You'll never credit what an awful notion she's come up with. She thinks...that is to say, she has decided...dash it all, Meg, she thinks that you and I should get leg-shackled!"

Meg blinked. "But of course you told her that you'd no desire to marry?"

"I tried to," Johnny said. "Honestly, Meg, I did! But when she said that she felt faint, and started to talk about how I should please myself and pay no regard to her feelings...! I hadn't the heart to continue."

"Well, you must just tell her that I am not interested, then," Meg said practically. "Tell her that you approached me, and that I turned you down."

"That will never work," Johnny said gloomily. "She read me a twenty-minute scold about how I must 'win' you; I fear that if I tell her I've failed, she'll just think that I didn't try."

"I see," Meg said. "What will you do, then?"

"I was thinking..." Johnny looked down at Meg uncertainly. "If you were really serious about not wanting a husband...?"

"I was," Meg said firmly. "I have thought the matter over most carefully, and I believe that it would suit me best to remain unmarried."

"Then why don't we pretend to be courting?" Johnny said eagerly. "Oh, I know it sounds mad, but only think about it, Meg! Seeing us apparently smelling of April and May would satisfy my mother, and keep Lady Carstairs from trying to push likely suitors onto you. Don't you see? It would answer to both our needs."

"I suppose," Meg said uncertainly. "But wouldn't your mother get suspicious when we never actually became betrothed?"

"I've already thought of that," Johnny said proudly. "If we tell her that you don't wish to become engaged until the end of your Season, she'd go back to the country. Mama hates London; once she was convinced that we were well and truly in love, she'd leave. Then I could just write to her and tell her that we'd fallen out."

"'Twould be far easier if you'd only tell her the truth now," Meg pointed out. "After all, she cannot compel you to wed."

"I know," Johnny said, crushed. "And I know that you must think me the most errant coward. But my mother has been so very good to me! My father died when I was very young, and Mama has tried so hard not to tie me to her apron strings. It makes it very difficult to refuse her the little she does ask of me."

"I see," Meg said. "Well, I'm willing to go along with the ruse, at least for the time being. As you said, 'twill benefit me, also." She smiled at Johnny.

"Thank you! And it won't be so very awful, I promise; I'll do my best to be an amusing companion." Johnny let go a gusty sigh. "I am relieved!" he said. "I wasn't sure that you'd agree, but I might have known—you're pluck to the backbone, Miss Margaret Sutton." He grinned. "Won't Wrendale laugh when I tell him!"

Meg's head snapped up. "No," she said flatly.

"What?"

"You will not tell Lord Wrendale anything about our little subterfuge," she said. Let Wrendale see, Meg thought, how little effect his homilies had on her!

"But why not?" Johnny asked. "He'd be the first to see the humour in it, that I'll be bound."

"No," Meg said again. "If you wish my help, Johnny, then you must promise me that the secret will stay between you and me. Wrendale must believe us to be in love, along with everyone else."

"Well, if you insist..." Johnny agreed uncertainly. "Though I can't think why you would!"

"I do insist," Meg said. "And if you need a reason, just call it a matter of pride."

CHAPTER FOUR

MEG DREW UP HER MOUNT and took a deep breath. "How wonderful it is to be out of doors," she said. "I have so missed riding." The day, after a misty start, had turned sunny and warm; the air smelled of flowers and green grass. Meg was thrilled to have finally convinced Aunt Sally to allow her an outing, but she was also a little dismayed by the number of people walking and driving through Hyde Park. She wished that she had thought to suggest that they ride earlier in the day, for it appeared that all of London had chosen this very moment to drive down Rotten Row and walk along the Serpentine. Still, she told herself, she would not repine! "I am so glad that Aunt Sally finally relented."

Roger Marden reined in his horse, a showy roan stallion, beside Meg; Meg's groom halted a discreet ten feet behind. "No more glad than I, I promise you," he said with a grin. "'Twas more than passing difficult to be only allowed to call on you for the correct half-hour each day, and to sit talking commonplaces with your dear aunt, estimable woman though she is."

Meg smiled at him. "It may have been a hardship for you, sir, but I promise you, 'twas a favour which I'll not soon forget. Were it not for you and dear Johnny Trevore, I should have spent the past weeks with nothing to distract me from the sound of my aunt's lamentations.''

"You know how I esteem Lady Carstairs," Marden said, "but in this case she was, I believe, overly protective. Insisting that you remain quietly at home for almost three weeks did no more than to postpone the inevitable. There is not as much talk as the dear lady believes about that unfortunate incident at Almack's, but what talk there is will die down the sooner now that you are being seen again. One cannot hide from gossip, you know. It is like some foul miasma, which creeps through closed doors and locked windows to do its evil work.''

"You speak as someone that knows the damage that gossip can do," Meg said, a little curious.

Marden shrugged. "No one is immune, my dear Miss Sutton," he said. "No one, that is, but my lord Wrendale and his like. They far prefer to wield gossip like a weapon, rather than to be its victim.''

Meg grimaced. They cantered on in silence for a moment, then Meg leaned forward in her saddle and said, "Look—is that not Johnny now, over there?'' She waved, but the distant riders apparently did not see her. "What a pretty lady he is riding with; who is she?''

Marden craned his neck, but the two figures had already disappeared from view. "I don't know," he said. "I didn't see them." He paused for a moment, then continued, "It was good of Trevore to call on you during the past few weeks. One would not have hoped to see such nicety of behaviour from him, considering his heritage.''

"He was all that is most kind," Meg said with a fond smile. "He called every day to regale me with the current on-dits, and quite refused to allow me to fall into the dismals.''

"You'll forgive me if I confess myself amazed,'' Marden said. "That the apple should fall so far from the tree. . . . Quite remarkable.''

"You must not speak against Johnny Trevore to me, if you please,'' Meg said with a mock frown. "We are the best of friends, I would have you know.''

"Indeed,'' Marden said. He felt the faintest twinge of alarm; he had not known that young Trevore had been so assiduous in his attentions.

"Do let us walk for a moment,'' Meg said. "Might we?'' She looked at Marden expectantly. "I am not so very familiar with Hyde Park, you know, as to disdain the chance to stroll its famous walkways.''

"Whatever my lady wishes,'' Marden said. He slid down, helped Meg from her horse, and gave both sets of reins to the groom. "Shall we?'' He extended his arm. He and Meg moved down a small path which turned into a more populated lane.

Meg had begun walking with a bounce in her step, but now she began to move more and more slowly. "It would appear,'' she said, "that Aunt Sally was rather more accurate in her prognostications than you were, Mr. Marden.''

Throughout the Park, members of the ton were strolling, riding and conversing; it was the most fashionable hour to be seen abroad. The air was filled with calls and polite laughter, and the lanes were crowded. Except, that is, around Meg and Roger Marden. A circle of silent emptiness surrounded them, through which no member of the ton strolled. No one called out to either Meg or Marden; no driver pulled up his phaeton or curricle to exchange greetings. Meg could see the averted looks, the sly glances and the whispering which went on behind delicately raised, gloved hands. She was particularly pained to notice several young gentlemen strolling together, all of whom had once been her devoted swains. At the sight of her they stopped, milled about uncertainly for a moment or two, then sidled uncomfortably away, all without speaking a word.

Marden, too, noticed the reaction of Meg's former suitors. He was hard put to hide his satisfaction; it would be the rare gentleman indeed that would pursue a fortune, however great, at the risk of incurring the displeasure of such a social lion as Wrendale, he thought.

Meg stopped, her cheeks burning. "I thought that I knew just how shallow and hypocritical London Society could be," she said. "It appears that I was wrong!"

"You mustn't let this cast you into despair..." Marden began.

"Despair?" Meg said. "Why, I am so furiously, overwhelming angry that I can barely speak! Who has asked me my side of the story, if you please? Who has asked me, or themselves, what Lord Wrendale might have done to compel me to leave him that night? No one! Wrendale is a peer, and I am simply a woman, of no account whatsoever. Therefore the fault must be mine."

"Not all of us believe that, Miss Sutton," Marden said softly.

Meg impulsively squeezed his arm. "Of course not," she said with a warm smile. "You have proven yourself to be my very good friend, Mr. Marden, and I shan't forget it, I promise you." She turned back to

survey the Park. "Neither shall I forget this," she said
grimly, waving her hand at the ton, so careful to ignore her. She stared for a moment longer, then sighed,
suddenly tired. "I find I've lost my taste for riding,"
she said. "Shall we go?"

Marden shook his head. "Will you allow yourself
to be cowed so easily?" he asked.

"What?"

Marden reached out and took her hand in his. "If
you'll take my advice, Miss Sutton, you won't allow
the gossipmongers to chase you back into hiding."

Meg's head snapped back. "They are not chasing
me anywhere," she said. "I have simply had my fill of
Hyde Park."

"Is that what they will say this evening, do you
think?" Marden asked. "When they are gathered at
Almack's, or at Lady Whatever's rout or ball, will
they say that Miss Sutton had had her fill of Hyde
Park? No, they will not." He leaned towards Meg.
"They will say," he said slowly, "that the young lady
tucked her tail between her legs and slunk away. They
will say that you were humiliated, and no better than
you deserve."

A dangerous light appeared in Meg's eyes. "Will
they, now?" she asked. "Well, we can't have that,
Marden. What can we do to make certain they know
that Meg Sutton was not frightened away?"

Marden tapped his riding crop against one buck-
skin-clad thigh. "How I wish that we could hurl our
defiance in their teeth," he said. "Jump on our
horses, perhaps, and gallop, *ventre a terre*, right
through their very midst. They couldn't ignore us
then."

"Done!" Meg cried, and started for the horses.

"Oh, but Miss Sutton, 'twould only make matters worse," Marden said earnestly. "Galloping in Hyde Park is considered to be ... well, it just isn't done."

"Is it not?" she said.

"Truly, my dear, I implore you to reconsider," Marden said carefully. "'Twould be most unwise."

With a martial light in her eyes, Meg Sutton jerked the reins of her mount out of the hands of the groom.

ACROSS THE PARK, Johnny Trevore and Patsy Billington were cantering gently across a clearing in the trees. "Now, aren't you glad you came?" Johnny said.

"It is a beautiful day," Patsy said. "And you have been very charming, I must allow." She favoured Johnny with a brilliant smile.

"Am I ever otherwise?" Johnny asked, and they both laughed. "Seriously, Patsy, it is too ridiculous of you to worry so about my reputation," Johnny went on. "After all, I am not some greenhorn when it comes to women."

"I can't help but feel—" Patsy began.

"Look, there's Wrendale," Johnny interrupted her. "Wren," he called. "Wren, over here!"

Lord Wrendale rode up on a magnificent black stallion which left Johnny gasping.

"I say," the younger man breathed. "What a beauty! Wherever did you find this treasure, Wren?"

"It's one of Hampton's cast-offs," Wrendale said. "I think rather highly of him myself." He turned his attention to Patsy. "Good day, Mrs. Billington," he said coolly.

"Good day, my lord," Patsy answered, her colour high. "A wonderful horse, in truth."

"Thank you." Wrendale did not smile.

An awkward silence fell on the trio; Patsy broke it, finally. "Johnny," she said, "I'm going to return home now. Why don't you stay and have a comfortable cose with your uncle? No, no," she added, as Johnny started to protest, "I have my groom with me, and he will see me safely home, I promise you."

"But, Patsy . . . !" Johnny said.

Patsy reached over and patted his arm. "Don't insult your uncle by acting as though his company were so onerous," she said. "How very rude he will think you! And I shall do very nicely. Perhaps I'll see you later, Johnny?" She straightened. "Good day, my lord," Patsy said, and rode off.

Wrendale watched her go in silence; Johnny was not so reticent. "You drove her off," he said to his uncle accusingly.

"Did I?" Wrendale asked indifferently.

Johnny's face flushed. "There was no need to be so dashed rude, Wren," he said. "You can't stop me from seeing her, you know."

"Very true," Wrendale acknowledged, as they rode slowly on. "But I should think that you would have more sense than to take Mrs. Billington riding in Hyde Park, and at a time when the news will, in all likelihood, get back to your mother before you've returned home."

"It's none of Mama's concern," Johnny said defiantly. "I am a grown man!"

"Once again, very true," Wrendale said. "But I think we would all have somewhat easier a time remembering that fact if you did not so often behave like a thoughtless child." Johnny gasped; Wrendale grinned at his nephew. "Yes, I know, a most outrageous thing to say. But really, halfling, you might at least have the courtesy to be discreet while your mother is in Town. 'Twould cost you nothing and set her mind very much more at rest.''

Johnny wavered between anger and remorse for a moment; remorse won. "You're right, of course," he acknowledged ruefully. "I shall have to make a special effort to mend fences with Mama, shan't I?''

"At the very least," Wrendale said. "Lavinia will..." He broke off, staring across the Park. "What is that infernal girl about now?" he exclaimed.

Johnny followed his uncle's eyes and bit back an oath. Meg Sutton was tearing across the sward, face flushed and smile bright, her horse running as hard as if it were in a race. All across Hyde Park scandalized observers stared, their mouths agape. As Wrendale and Johnny watched, Meg touched the horse with her crop, urging the beast to greater and greater speed.

Wrendale had spent a very uncomfortable few weeks because of Margaret Sutton. At first, after she had stormed off the dance floor at Almack's, leaving him looking the fool, Wrendale had been furious. One or two of his cronies had been unwise enough to twig him, that night, about making improper advances towards the girl; Wrendale smiled grimly and thought that those gentlemen would never again be so brave as to comment to him on his behaviour.

But as the days had passed, and Wrendale's anger had had time to cool, he had begun to wonder uncomfortably if he had not deserved Miss Sutton's scorn. He had made his decision to help Lady Carstairs keep an eye out for the girl, and had jumped right into the task; he wondered now if he hadn't gone slightly beyond the bounds in his desire to help. He could not fathom what it was about Miss Sutton which made him behave so ham-handedly whenever he was around her, but so it was. The more he thought on it, the more he realized that his comments to Miss Sutton would have been better left unsaid.

"Stay here, Johnny," Wrendale ordered his nephew, and dug his heels into the flanks of his mount. Wrendale's horse flew across the Park; within seconds he had pulled parallel to Meg and was running neck and neck with her. The pair crossed half the Park before Wrendale shouted to Meg to pull up.

Reluctant as Meg was to pay any heed to anything Wrendale might say, she was already regretting the impulsive action which had made her set her horse in motion. She slowed her mount, and came to a halt just as she and Wrendale reached one of the carriage roads. Wrendale startled her by speaking to the inhabitants of one of the carriages which had stopped to watch Meg fly across the Park.

"Ah, Lady Lieven," Wrendale said, "you have caught me out, I see."

The renowned Countess Lieven, one of the coldest and most haughty of the Patronesses of Almack's, inclined her head slightly to Wrendale, and fixed Meg with an unblinking stare. "Indeed, my lord?" she said. "How so?"

"I'm afraid that I have encouraged Miss Sutton to be very naughty," Wrendale said with an easy smile. "When she questioned the speed of my newest horse, I challenged her to a race on the spot, to prove the merits of the beast."

"It is not *comme il faut,* my lord," the countess said humourlessly. "You should have known better."

"I should indeed," Wrendale said. "But I fear that I allowed my sporting blood to overrule my head. Say that I am forgiven?"

"Of course," the countess said with an icy smile.

"And of course you will not blame poor Miss Sutton for rising to my challenge? I'm ashamed to say that I made it impossible for her to refuse."

"Miss Sutton must be held to be responsible for her own actions, I think," the countess said, with no visible signs of thawing.

"Indeed, you are quite right, my lady," Meg said proudly. "I would scorn to blame my behaviour—or my misbehaviour!—on any other than myself."

The other occupant of the carriage spoke up. "Very well spoken," Lady Jersey said approvingly. "There is nothing so refreshing, I think, as a young miss that does not hide her teeth. Spare me any more of these milk-and-water damsels, if you please! I find their insipidity truly enervating." She leaned forward in the carriage, her expression mischievous. "Tell me, my dear," she said. "Since you are so loath to blame others for your own mistakes, pray explain to me how it is that you came to quarrel so publicly with my lord Wrendale at Almack's."

"Sally!" the countess said quellingly.

"That, in truth, was my doing," Wrendale said. "I am the rudest man in London, am I not? I overstepped the bounds of what is polite, and Miss Sutton responded most firmly, no more than that."

"Do tell," Lady Jersey breathed avidly. "Does he speak the truth, my dear?" She fixed a bright glance on Meg.

Meg shifted uncomfortably in her saddle. Reluctant as she was to appear friendly with Wrendale, Meg

was not unmindful of how important it was to keep
the favour of the Patronesses of Almack's. If she
wished to find any enjoyment in her stay in London
she must be wary of causing any further talk; this
morning's experience in the Park had taught her that
much! And Wrendale had been only truthful in taking the blame onto his own shoulders. "I would say,"
she said carefully, "that his lordship forgot that he was
Lady Carstairs's old acquaintance, and not mine. He
no doubt intended to be avuncular, but..." She trailed
to a halt.

Lady Jersey gave a hoot of high-pitched laughter.
"'Avuncular,' indeed!" she chuckled. "You are put
firmly in your place, aren't you, Wrendale?" She returned her attention to Meg. "Well, I daresay we shall
all forgive you, if Wrendale does," Lady Jersey said.
"Shan't we, my friend?"

The Countess Lieven seemed ill disposed to assent,
but finally she agreed grudgingly, "I suppose that we
might allow Miss Sutton one mistake."

"As long as you understand, my dear, that one
chance is all you will get," Lady Jersey continued, no
longer smiling. "Pray do not be tiresome again."

Meg nodded, suitably chastened. The Patronesses
drove away as Johnny Trevore rode up and joined
them.

"Meg, what were you thinking of?" Johnny said
indignantly. "Mean to say, are you quite set on ruin-
ing yourself?"

"Enough, Johnny," Wrendale said quietly. "I do
believe that Miss Sutton has realized the folly of her
actions."

Meg bristled. "I would remind you, my lord..."

Wrendale continued speaking as though he had not heard her. "Johnny, would you be so good as to escort Miss Sutton home? I feel confident that she has had quite enough of Hyde Park for one day."

In all honesty, Meg could not say that she was not anxious to leave this afternoon's events behind her, but she was determined not to allow Lord Wrendale to order her life. "I came riding this afternoon with Mr. Marden," she said. "He will see me home, thank you."

"You need have no fears on that score," Wrendale said. "I shall personally make all right with Mr. Marden. In fact, I am most anxious to speak to him."

At that moment, Roger Marden rode up to join the group. "Miss Sutton! Are you in need of my services?"

Wrendale turned towards Marden, his expression unreadable. "I was just telling Miss Sutton," he said, "that you would understand perfectly if she allowed my nephew to see her home, Mr. Marden. You and I have matters to discuss. Is that not so?"

Marden met Wrendale's gaze squarely; curious about what the peer might want with him, he nodded. "Of course," he said. "That is, if you do not object, Miss Sutton?"

Meg looked at the two men, puzzled by the tension between them, then held out her hand to Marden. "Thank you for what could have been a perfect day," she said with a rueful smile.

"I assure you, my dear Miss Sutton, the next time it shall be," Marden said. He bowed in his saddle as Meg and Johnny rode off.

"My curiosity is stirred, Mr. Marden," Wrendale said. He urged his horse into a walk; Marden rode slowly along beside him. "How did Miss Sutton come to be so imprudent as to gallop through Hyde Park?"

Marden shrugged. "I fear she is a headstrong girl," he said. "Possessed of quite a fiery temper, in fact."

"Yes," Lord Wrendale said, disliking Marden more by the moment. "And how bright a fire does burn when it is poked!"

"Alas, the lady needed no encouragement," Marden returned. "She was determined to make her mark, so to speak."

"And of course you did not feel it was your place to provide the cool voice of reason?" Wrendale said.

"May I ask what concern this is of yours, my lord?" Marden asked. "Surely Miss Sutton is not a dependent of yours, nor any connection whatsoever?"

"I shall not bore you by explaining my concerns," Wrendale said coolly. "Suffice it to say that I take an...avuncular interest in the young lady." Wrendale stifled a wry smile at the word. "An interest which would compel me, if forced, to take extremely strong measures against anyone who might try to do her harm." He met Marden's gaze blandly. "Anyone at all."

"We can only hope, then, that no one will be so foolish," Marden said, matching his lordship's dispassionate tone. "How flattered Miss Sutton must be by your championship of her, my lord."

Wrendale chuckled. "Miss Sutton does not know of it, and would not believe you if you told her." He met Marden's eyes, and the chuckle died. "Think well on what I've said, Mr. Marden. I shall not say it again."

Marden's expression was calm as he watched the peer ride away; he gave no sign of the anger which churned within his breast. What a fool he had been to think that Wrendale might want Meg for himself! It was clear that Wrendale did, indeed, have an eye to Meg Sutton's fortune, but not for himself—rather, for his nephew, the accursed Johnny Trevore! This also explained why Johnny had taken such pains to stand Meg's friend during her recent, apparently now forgotten, estrangement from Wrendale, and why Wrendale had just made such an effort to try to restore the Sutton girl in the eyes of the ton. Wrendale might be a stickler for the social niceties, but not, it appeared, to the extent of depriving his nephew of a fortune.

Roger Marden kicked his horse into a walk. He was damned if he would allow a callow fool like Wrendale's nephew to steal such a plum from under his very nose. *Beware, Johnny Trevore,* he thought. *You shall rue the day that you ever decided to woo Meg Sutton!*

JOHNNY TREVORE SHOOK his head sadly. "You had best beware, Meg," he said. "You came very close today to total ruin." He and Meg rode close together, as the streets were crowded.

Meg scowled. "You are beginning to sound more and more like your uncle Wrendale."

"You have good cause to be grateful to Wrendale," Johnny snapped. "Don't you realize he saved your reputation for you? And he didn't have to, you know. He could easily have stood by and watched you gallop your way to perdition."

Meg shifted uncomfortably in her saddle. Wrendale had gone out of his way to make all right for Meg with the Patronesses and, as Johnny pointed out, he had been under no obligation to do so. "Well," she said, unwilling to admit that Johnny was right, "that may be so. But it was still an interference in my life, however well intentioned it might have been."

"How very gracious of you," Johnny said sarcastically. "And how sorry my uncle will be to know that he has offended you!" Johnny rode along silently for a moment, oblivious to the traffic and pedestrians which filled the London streets. "It was only to be expected, of course, that you should find yourself in trouble again," he said after a time. "If you will associate with the likes of Roger Marden and his crony Fortesque...."

"Mr. Marden is my friend, Johnny," Meg said stiffly, "as much as you are."

"Well, I like that," Johnny said indignantly. "Comparing my friendship to that of a bounder like Marden! Why, the man's no better than a card sharp."

Meg was taken aback. "How do you know?" she asked sharply. "Have you seen him cheat at play?"

"No," Johnny admitted, "but I've heard—from more than one gentleman!—that Marden is a little too lucky."

Meg's lips tightened. She remembered what Marden had said about gossip, and how she had suspected that he, too, was the victim of vicious tale bearers. "I'll believe no such lies of my friend," she said. "Mr. Marden has been very kind, and I am grateful to him. And I take it very ill in you, Johnny, to tell me such lies about him!"

"Dash it all, Meg, if someone don't take you in hand, you'll find yourself at point non plus," Johnny grumbled.

Meg's head snapped up. "No one," she said clearly, "will ever 'take me in hand' again. My father did that for too long, and in too strict a fashion."

Johnny hesitated for a moment, then asked, "Was it very bad, Meg?" When Meg looked at him, he added hastily, "'Tis just that you've mentioned your father several times, and . . . well, the memories don't seem to be happy ones. Don't talk about it, though, if you'd rather not."

Meg blinked back sudden tears. However much Johnny might have annoyed her, going on and on about Marden, she could never doubt that he was most truly her friend. "Oh, Johnny," she said, "how can I make you understand what it was like? To picture myself here, riding along home with you after an outing in the Park, would have been a fevered dream while my father was alive. I used to yearn so for some kind of freedom; to be allowed to go shopping, perhaps, or to walk somewhere other than on the grounds of my father's estate. . . ."

"It can't have been that bad, Meg," Johnny said reasonably. "Good Lord, you make it sound as though you were in gaol."

Meg's expression was bleak. "Towards the end of my father's life, I was," she said simply. "I went nowhere; I saw no one but my father and the household staff. Until I came to London, it had been literally years since I had met anyone new, or conversed with a gentleman."

"I had no idea," Johnny said, appalled. "I've no wish to insult you, Meg, but it sounds as though your father were . . . well, not quite right, if you know what I mean!"

"You might say that," Meg agreed. "Papa was always a little eccentric, but towards the end he became obsessed with the notion that a fortune-hunter would sweep me off my feet, or a kidnapper hold me to ransom." She gave a bitter laugh. "He had no idea how I used to long to be kidnapped—just for the change!"

"It surprises me," Johnny said, "that you are not frightened of people. One would think, after your experience, that you would be the most shrinking of violets. But that, my dear Meg, you most certainly are not."

"I think it was the reading," Meg said thoughtfully. "One thing I must admit is that my father did allow me to order what books I pleased; I was able to read of subjects that most well-raised young ladies would be forbidden. My reading provided me with a very broad view." She met Johnny's gaze. "So you mustn't believe that I'm some innocent babe that must be protected," she added earnestly. "I do know rather more of the world than you might think."

"You'll forgive me, Meg," Johnny said gently, "if I say that you have not demonstrated any great talent for negotiating the shoals of London society."

Meg smiled ruefully. "It is more difficult than I expected it to be," she admitted. "There are so many rules!"

"That is why it is foolish of you to be too proud to accept a helping hand from time to time," Johnny said. "My uncle went out of his way to help you today. Can you not admit that?"

Meg bit her lip, then sighed. "Yes," she said. "I owe him my thanks, I suppose."

"And will you stay away from Roger Marden?" Johnny pressed.

"There, you go too far, Johnny," Meg said mulishly. "Mr. Marden has proven himself to be my very good friend."

"I only hope," Johnny muttered to himself, "that that may continue to hold true." *But somehow,* he thought obstinately, *I doubt it!*

CHAPTER FIVE

ROGER MARDEN STEPPED out onto the steps of his townhouse. He pulled at the lapels of his frock coat, adjusted the tilt of his curly-brimmed beaver hat and went down the stairs. The fenced square of grass across from his home was filled with nannies and small children taking advantage of the beautiful spring weather, and the street vendors were out in force, cajoling one and all to buy their varied wares. Sauntering down the street, Marden gently swung his cane and thought what a beautiful morning it was.

Roger Marden was feeling very cheerful this morning. He had been disconcerted when he first realized that Wrendale wanted to make a match between Meg Sutton and Johnny Trevore, but a period of calm reflection had restored his confidence. Whether Wrendale wanted Meg for himself or for his nephew was immaterial; Wrendale would still let the girl, and her fortune, go if he felt that Meg was too great a social liability. So Marden's plan would still work; if he encouraged Meg to behave badly and to give the ton a disgust of her, he could still win the prize. It would not be easy, Marden thought. He would be compelled to move very carefully, lest Wrendale realize what Marden was up to and take action against him. But his latest notion might settle the whole matter before

Wrendale's interference ever became an issue! He chuckled softly to himself.

"Marden!"

Roger Marden turned to see Willy Fortesque hurrying up. "Good morning, Willy," he said. "What's to do?"

"Lord, I've been chasing you for two blocks," Fortesque complained. "I'm sweating so much that my points are starting to wilt." He anxiously raised a hand to the high points of his shirt collar which had, indeed, begun to droop.

"A tragedy," Marden sneered. "Perhaps you should hurry right home and let your valet succour you."

"Oh, no," Fortesque said. "I've a matter to discuss with you. You've been avoiding me, I know it. That's why I'm here so infernally early, to catch you before you could run off."

Marden shrugged. "I haven't been avoiding you," he said. "I've just been rather busy of late."

"Yes, busy chasing that Sutton girl," Fortesque said indignantly. "I call it shabby of you, Roger, to steal her from beneath my very nose."

Marden gave a hoot of rude laughter. "I didn't steal her from you, Willy," he said. "The girl wants nothing to do with you."

"She might have, if you hadn't poisoned her mind against me," Fortesque said.

"You need blame no one else for Miss Sutton's dislike of you, Willy," Marden said. "That bit of work may be laid squarely at your own door. She'll never entertain your suit, not in a thousand lifetimes."

"And you think she'll have you?" Fortesque said. "I shouldn't wager any of your blunt on it, if I were you, Roger."

"Oh, she'll have me," Marden said, a grim tone in his voice. "She'll have me, one way or the other."

"My lord Wrendale may have something to say to that," Fortesque said.

Marden stopped walking and turned to look at his friend, eyes narrowed. "What do you mean by that remark?"

"I'm not such a fool as you clearly think me," Fortesque said. "I've noticed the way Johnny Trevore is pursuing the Sutton chit. And you may be sure, Roger," Fortesque added, nodding his head wisely, "that it was Wrendale's idea to begin with. Lord, Johnny Trevore don't want to get leg-shackled! He'd be just as happy to spend all his time, and money, on la Billington. Mark my words, my friend, it's his lordship who's piping the tune."

"How very perspicacious of you, Willy," Roger Marden said. "And you're quite right—you aren't as great a fool as I thought you!" Marden resumed walking. "Do you know," he said slowly, "I do believe that I may be able to use you in l'affaire de Sutton."

"Why should I help you?" Fortesque said bitterly. "After the way you cut me out with her, there's no earthly reason why I should lift a finger to help you."

"But of course there is," Marden replied. "Money, my dear Willy, and lots of it. If you help me to win the lady, I am prepared to be very generous with you, very generous indeed."

"I don't believe it," Fortesque said flatly. "I've never seen the colour of your money yet, Roger, and I daresay that I never shall."

Roger Marden sighed, and took out his pocket-book. "Will fifty pounds convince you that I'm serious?" he asked.

"I should say so!" Willy Fortesque snatched the money out of Marden's hand before he could withdraw it. "What do you want me to do?"

"Watch her, Willy," Marden said. "I want to know everywhere that she goes, and everyone that she sees. I don't want Meg Sutton or Lady Carstairs to so much as take a step or speak to a servant without my knowing about it. Do you understand?"

Fortesque nodded eagerly. "Anything else?"

Marden shook his head. "Go and start now," he said. "I'll see you later on."

"And what will you be doing?"

Roger Marden smiled. "I," he said, "shall be mounting an opening sortie in my campaign against young Master Trevore. Wish me luck, Willy. Though I doubt," he added smoothly, "if I shall need it!"

LAVINIA TREVORE RAISED a hand to her mouth and yawned delicately. "I can't think why you rise at such an ungodly hour," she complained. "It cannot be good for one's health to eat so early in the day." Lavinia sat at one end of the breakfast table, charmingly attired in a lavender morning robe.

Watching her, Wrendale wondered not for the first time if Lavinia insisted on dressing in mourning shades so long after the death of her husband as a sign of respect for his memory, or because she knew that the blacks, lavenders and soft greys of widowhood suited her colouring so very well. "There was no need for you to rise and breakfast with me, Lavinia," he said. "My people would have been more than happy to bring you a tray in your room, whenever you were ready for it."

"Ah, well," Lavinia sighed. "A guest must adapt herself to her host's habits, however difficult it may be."

"And the fact that Johnny is joining me for breakfast had no bearing on your decision?" Wrendale quirked an eyebrow at Lavinia.

"It will be pleasant to see my son," Lavinia admitted with dignity. "'Tis so rare for me to get the chance to share a meal with Johnny." She busied herself with her tea and toast points. "I can't think," she continued too casually, "why Johnny does not simply reside here with you, Wrendale. After all, one man rattling round in this enormous house . . . well, it's absurd."

"That may be, but I think Johnny is very comfortable in his rooms on Green Street," Wrendale said.

"Yes, but Grosvenor Square would be so much better an address for him to live at," Lavinia said persuasively. "And you must allow, Wrendale, Johnny would never have got himself involved with that Billington woman if he had been living here with you."

"But of course he would," Wrendale said. "My dear Lavinia, do you honestly think that Johnny would pay any heed at all to me if I were so muddleheaded as to try to run his life? I assure you he would not, whether he lived here or in Green Street."

"You just don't want to be bothered with him," Lavinia said accusingly. "You think he'd be a nuisance if he lived here."

"On the contrary, I shouldn't mind at all if Johnny chose to make his home with me," Wrendale said calmly. "As you pointed out, this house is large enough to accommodate a score of people and still allow them all ample privacy. But I respect the independence which makes Johnny want to live in bachelor digs. 'Tis healthy for a lad his age to strike out on his own."

"You would not feel so if you were a parent," Lavinia said darkly. "The worries which we mothers are subjected to!"

"Unfortunately, Lavinia, some of those worries are of your own making," Wrendale said. "This business with Patsy Billington, for example—"

Lavinia held up a hand. "I shan't quarrel with you again on that subject," she said with a tight smile. "I am all too aware of how differently men and women regard these matters." She sipped her tea, and changed the topic. "I must thank you, Wrendale," she said, "for your efforts yesterday on Miss Sutton's behalf. When I heard that you had made things right for the foolish child with Lady Jersey—and that awful Countess Lieven!—I was most agreeably surprised in you."

"I didn't do it for you, Lavinia," Wrendale said flatly.

"Well, of course you didn't," Lavinia said. "But to have such a care for Johnny's interests is more than I expected of you, Wrendale, I tell you that to your head."

"I didn't do it for Johnny, either," Wrendale said. "As you know, I think that this notion of yours to make a match between Johnny and Miss Sutton is nonsense."

"Why did you, then?" Lavinia asked, colour high. "Never tell me that it was just a random charitable instinct; I'll not believe you!"

"Once I realized that it was my own fault Miss Sutton left me on the dance floor that night, I knew that I should have to make amends to her," Wrendale said.

"Well, whatever motivated you, 'twas very well done indeed," Lavinia said. "It would never do for Miss Sutton to be permanently shunned by the ton."

"I do wish that you would give up trying to push Johnny and Miss Sutton together," Wrendale said in irritation. "It's quite hopeless, you know, Lavinia. I don't believe they've the slightest interest in each other romantically."

Lavinia smiled broadly. "We shall see, shan't we, Wrendale?" she asked, then rose to her feet. "Johnny!" She held out both her hands. "Good morning, love."

Johnny Trevore had followed Stubbs, Wrendale's butler, into the breakfast room. John did not look well; eyes red and complexion grey, he gave every indication of having spent a night on the Town, hot to hand and on the toddle. That he had ended the night castaway, if not shot in the neck, seemed certain to his uncle.

"Good morning, Mama, Wren," Johnny said. He glanced at the silver dishes piled on the sideboard, shuddered and lowered himself carefully into a chair.

"Good heavens, Johnny, whatever is wrong with you?" Lavinia asked sharply as she poured her son's tea. "You do not look at all well. Are you ill, my dear?"

"I'm fine, Mama," Johnny said listlessly. "Just a little tired."

"This," Lavinia said, "is precisely what I've been telling you, John Trevore. Your style of living must change, for the sake of your health if nothing else."

"Lavinia, not before breakfast, I beg you," Wrendale said pleasantly. "Wrangling is so very bad for the digestion, is it not?"

"You shan't silence me, Wrendale," Lavinia said dramatically. "This constant racketing about Town shall be the death of you, Johnny. And I, for one, do not intend to stand idly by and allow it!"

"You are making far too much of this, Mama," Johnny said, engaging in a valiant effort to sit up and look alert. "It's a sad day when a man can't go a little too hard without being accused of being a dashed reprobate."

"You will not use such vulgarities in my presence, if you please," his mother said coldly. "And if you think that your appearance this morning is the first time you've caused me disquiet since I came to Town, then you are sadly mistaken." Lavinia glared at Johnny. "Need I repeat to you all the unsavoury gossip I have heard about you of late?"

"Mama, please . . ." Johnny began.

"Don't 'Mama' me," Lavinia snapped. "You have made yourself the object of the most unpleasant kind of talk, Johnny, as I'm sure I need not tell you. Your choice of female companionship has cast a shadow on an old and respected name. I can only be grateful that your father is not alive to see how you have disgraced the family."

"Really, Mama, you exaggerate," Johnny protested. "I've done nothing to shame my name."

Before Lavinia could respond, Wrendale held up both hands. "To repeat myself, I must insist that we not indulge in a fit of high dramatics at table," he said. "May we change the course of this conversation?"

Lavinia struggled with herself for a long moment, then said, "Of course, my lord." She stressed the title.

Wrendale laughed aloud. "That has put me in my place, hasn't it, dear sister?"

Lavinia ignored her brother-in-law. "Tell me, my dear," she said to Johnny, "have you seen much of Miss Sutton of late?"

"Ah . . . yes," Johnny said. "I have." He suddenly seemed fascinated by the contents of his teacup.

"And?" Lavinia prompted, watching her son closely.

"And I like her very much," Johnny said uncomfortably. "She's a taking little thing."

"What a common way to describe such a charming young lady," Lavinia said lightly. "But I must tell you, Johnny, I heartily agree with you. Now there is a friendship which can do you naught but good."

"At the very least," Wrendale murmured.

"And you do plan to further your acquaintance with the young lady?" Lavinia pressed.

"I do," Johnny said; he did not look up.

"Very well, then!" Lavinia said, shooting a triumphant glance at Wrendale. She rose to her feet. "I'll leave you two gentlemen to finish your breakfast in peace," she said. "For myself, I simply must do some shopping. I fear that my wardrobe has become sadly out of date since last I was in Town!" With a wave, she left them.

Johnny groaned as soon as Lavinia left the room. "Lord, Wren," he confessed, "I've such a head!"

"So I suspected," his uncle answered. "But you handled yourself tolerably well, halfling. Indeed, I never would have thought you capable of such mendacity in your condition."

"What do you mean?" Johnny asked uneasily.

"My dear boy, you do realize that you left your mother with the impression that you mean to woo Meg Sutton?" Wrendale said. "I can sympathize with your motives; 'twas the only way to blunt your mother's ire. But it won't wash, I'm afraid. Sooner or later she will realize that it's all a hum."

"What if I tell you that it wasn't a hum?"

"Really," Wrendale said. One mobile brow flew up.

"Meg is a diamond of the first water," Johnny said defensively. "Any man would count himself lucky to win such a girl."

"Next you'll be telling me that it was love at first sight," Wrendale scoffed. "Give over, Johnny, do."

"Well, what if it was?" Johnny retorted. "I should think you'd be happy about it. You were just telling me that it's my responsibility to marry."

"And you just told me," Wrendale reminded him gently, "that you'd no intention of stepping into parson's mousetrap."

"Dash it all, mayn't a man change his mind?" Johnny said indignantly.

"Of course he may," Wrendale said. "But typically, it takes more than a pair of weeks for the change to occur. Tell me the truth, lad—what's really behind this sudden interest in Miss Sutton?"

Johnny rose to his feet and threw down his serviette. "It's bad enough," he said bitterly, "that a man's mother feels she may interrogate him about the way he lives. But I call it too much, Wren, when you join in the chorus!''

"Come now, John, don't you think you're overreacting?" Wrendale said reasonably.

"If you'll forgive me, sir, I have matters to attend to," Johnny said. "I bid you good day." With that, Johnny Trevore turned and stamped out of the breakfast room.

Wrendale watched Johnny leave in something akin to astonishment. It wasn't like Johnny to be so defensive, or to take offence so easily. Something, Wrendale thought, was most definitely afoot!

PATSY BILLINGTON WAS sleeping. She lay curled up in sheets of the palest pink silk, sheets which Lavinia Trevore would have stigmatized as "positively indecent!" The brazen nature of her bed linens did not appear to trouble Patsy; she slept deeply, only stirring to reach a hand out to pull up her coverlet. When her hand did not encounter the fluffy down cover, she opened her eyes, only to gasp in shock.

Roger Marden was standing over her, holding her coverlet back with one hand, examining her body through his quizzing glass. "Ah, Patsy," he said, "still such a beautiful figure. How do you do it, at your age?"

Patsy skittered backwards into the corner of the bed farthest from Marden, clutching the sheets before her. "What are you doing here?" she cried. "How did you get in?"

Marden dropped the blanket and held up a key. "I fear that I forgot to return this to you, my dear," he said. "So, as your maid was not at home, I let myself in."

"Get out," Patsy said. "Out!"

"As you well know, Patsy," Marden said, settling himself into the chair before her dressing-table, "I come and go as I please. You can't have forgotten all my little ways so soon?"

Patsy paled. She had not forgotten Marden's habits; she doubted if she ever would.

On the night that Patsy Billington met Roger Marden, he had gone out of his way to charm her. Between protectors, Patsy had enjoyed what she assumed would be an evening of harmless flirtation, and had readily agreed when Marden offered to see her home; she had even invited him in for a brandy. Marden had drunk his brandy, then calmly informed Patsy that from that time on, she would be his mistress. When Patsy had coldly refused, Marden had set out to convince her that she would be most unwise to spurn him. He had convinced her. For the year that Patsy was Marden's mistress, she had lived in constant fear of him, and learned, to her regret, that he always got what he wanted, by fair means or foul. When Marden had finally told Patsy that he had tired of her, she had been dizzy with relief.

Marden chuckled softly to himself. "I see that you have not forgotten me," he said.

Patsy judged it prudent not to answer him. She snatched up her dressing-gown and wrapped herself in its voluminous folds.

Marden stared through his quizzing glass at her bed. "Pink silk sheets," he said. "What a typically juvenile conceit—I have no doubt that Trevore compared you to Botticelli's Venus when he gave them to you?"

Patsy flushed; Johnny had indeed lavished compliments on her to go with the bed linens. "Johnny is very generous," she said defiantly. "And I love the sheets."

"I don't doubt that," Marden said. "When did you ever object to a gentleman spending money on you?"

"What do you want with me, Roger?" Patsy asked.

"You wound me, my pet," Marden said. "After all we have been to each other, did you not know that I would always take an interest in how you are and what you are about?" Patsy tried to repress a shudder. "Young Johnny Trevore, for example," Marden continued. "Does he treat you well? Are you happy with him?"

"He has been most kind," Patsy said, watching Marden warily. "He's a very sweet boy."

"And truly enamoured of you, as I understand it." He heaved an exaggerated sigh. "How it takes one back, to one's own first love—the excessive language, the indiscreet letters, the expensive gifts.... You will laugh to hear it, Patsy, but with my first mistress, I actually wrote to her every hour on the hour for a time. I can't imagine that Trevore is quite that besotted, though."

Stung, Patsy retorted, "He has written to me quite often, I would have you know, and given me the most exquisite gifts."

"How very nice," Roger Marden said blandly.

Patsy stood, her dressing-gown pulled tightly about her. "Roger, what do you want with me?" she asked again.

"Actually, it's Johnny Trevore that I want to talk to you about," Marden said. "I saw the dear boy last evening; he is not looking well, Patsy, not well at all. I do believe that it would be good for him to leave

London for a time, to regain his health in more salubrious surroundings.''

"You must be mad, Roger," Patsy said scornfully. "Why, the boy is the picture of rude good health."

"'Twould be most unfortunate if Johnny's continued presence in Town had an adverse affect on his well-being," Marden said softly.

Patsy did not miss Marden's implied threat. "What have you against him, Roger?" she asked sharply. "Surely he has never done you any harm?"

"My dear Patsy, I am concerned only for his health," Roger said.

"Well, there is no way that I could get him to leave London, even if I wanted to," Patsy said. "He indulges me, certainly, but not to that extent."

"Most unfortunate," Marden said. "Most unfortunate indeed." He took up his hat and cane, and started towards the doorway. "If you have any affection at all for the boy, Patsy," he paused on the threshold to say, "you would do well to persuade him to rusticate for a time. Else, I may be forced to find less pleasant means to ensure his absence."

Patsy Billington could only watch Marden leave in silence, convinced that poor Johnny had somehow made himself a terrible, terrible enemy.

CHAPTER SIX

MEG SUTTON PUT DOWN her sewing with a sigh. "I do hope I'll finish on time," she said. "They're expecting the baby any day now, and I've still one whole side to stitch."

"Were it not for your own foolishness," Lady Sally Carstairs grumbled, "you would have better things to do than embroider a blanket for a parlour maid's child."

"Mary is more than a servant to me," Meg said. "She was my constant companion when my father was alive—the closest thing to a friend I had. Had I a thousand things to do, I would still find time to make this blanket for her baby." She smoothed her work with one hand. "Her wedding was the only social event my father ever let me attend," she said. "She married the under-groom, you know. They had the wedding in my father's barn, and there was food and games and a fiddler for dancing afterwards. We had such fun!"

"It absolutely sickens me," said Sally crossly, "that after living such an...unnatural life, now that you finally have the chance to enjoy yourself, what must you do but ruin the whole thing? There are times, Margaret Sutton, when I could just shake you."

Meg was saved the necessity of answering Aunt Sally's reproaches by the entrance of Winters, the butler. "My lord Wrendale has arrived, my lady," he said. "Are you at home?"

Sally bounced to her feet. "But of course we are," she said. "Go and show Lord Wrendale up, Winters. But give us just a moment first, to collect ourselves." When the servant bowed and left the room, Sally turned to Meg. "He's really forgiven you!" she exclaimed. "I dared not hope... but it must be true."

"I don't want to see him," Meg said mulishly.

Lady Sally Carstairs stared at her, aghast. "But you must," she said. "After what happened in the Park yesterday—yes, well may you stare! You did not see fit to tell me how kind Wrendale had been to you, did you? But I heard of it none the less, and I warn you, Meg, I'll tolerate no more of these crotchets. You are very much in my lord's debt, and you know it."

"You're right, of course," Meg admitted slowly. She could not say exactly why she was so reluctant to acknowledge Wrendale's service to her, but she was. "I suppose I've no choice but to receive him."

"That's better," Sally said. She hurried over and pulled at Meg's skirt, then straightened the ribbon threaded through her charge's curls. "There," she said. "Had I known that Wrendale was coming, I would have had you change your dress, but you will do very nicely, I think."

"Aunt Sally," Meg asked, "may I ask you a favour?"

Sally, her good humour restored, said, "Of course, my pet. What is it?"

"Let me see him alone. If I must humble myself to Wrendale, I would prefer not to have an audience while I do it."

"'Tis the greatest foolishness to be speaking of humbling yourself to him," Sally said. "All that is necessary is for you to thank him prettily for his services to you in the Park, and to beg his pardon for that unfortunate incident at Almack's."

"But I may do it alone?" Meg pressed.

Sally wavered for a moment, then capitulated. "Very well," she said. "You may tell Wrendale that I have been delayed for a few moments." She patted Meg's shoulder, then slipped out of the drawing-room.

Meg stood very straight, her hands behind her back, as Wrendale entered the room. "Good day, my lord," she said resolutely, then stopped. "Oh!"

Wrendale held out a delicate bouquet of spring flowers. "For you," he said. He watched as Meg hesitantly took the nosegay; her face was a study in confusion.

"Is it not bad of me to put you in such a quandary?" he asked with a sympathetic grin. "You greet me, full of righteous disdain, ready to freeze me with a word, I have no doubt, only to be thrown off your guard by a gift of flowers. It is despicable of me, I'll admit. But if I am to restore myself to your good graces, I must take any opportunity I have to ingratiate myself with you."

"Pray do not be absurd, my lord," Meg said stiffly. "They are very beautiful. Thank you." She laid the bouquet on a table.

Wrendale watched her for a moment; uncomfortably aware of his eyes on her, Meg began to fiddle with her needlework.

"I've come to most humbly beg your pardon," Wrendale said finally. "It was inexcusable for me to provoke you in the way I did at Almack's that night.

Everything you said was true; I was ill-mannered and insufferable."

Meg's head snapped up. "You were?"

"I was." Wrendale grimaced wryly. "Mind you, I cannot recommend it as a way to endear yourself to the ton, but I have come to see that you were perfectly justified in your actions."

Meg let out a breath. "I'm sorry, too," she said, with what Wrendale believed to be the first genuine smile she had ever directed at him. "I lost my temper. Despite your... provocation, I should never have allowed my anger to get the better of me."

"Are we restored to perfect amity, then?" Wrendale said.

"There is one more thing, my lord," Meg said as she squared her shoulders, "I must thank you for everything you did at the Park yesterday. I have been brought to see that you went out of your way to restore me in the eyes of the ton and, most particularly, the Patronesses."

"'You have been brought to see...','" Wrendale repeated. "I daresay that means that you have been subjected to a bear garden jaw from either my nephew or your chaperon, possibly both. My dear girl, how can you forgive me, when I've opened you up to such odiously tiresome lectures?"

Meg gurgled with laughter. "They both were rather forthcoming on the subject," she admitted, "but they were right, and so I own."

Wrendale bowed his head. "I thank you," he said, "but I must point out that all I did was to tell the Patronesses the truth."

"The truth?" Meg said. "That you had challenged me to a race?"

Wrendale shrugged. "Well, perhaps a little more than the truth," he allowed. "But I owed it to you to repair the breach between you and the rest of London Society. Had it not been for me, you would never have been in social purdah in the first place."

"Yes, but I went from bad to worse," Meg said. "I knew that it was wrong to gallop in Hyde Park, but somehow I couldn't seem to stop myself. This awful temper of mine...!"

He opened his mouth to speak, then closed it. Wrendale had seen Roger Marden watching Meg ride away, and he was convinced that Marden had somehow provoked Meg into disobeying the stricture against galloping. However, the accord between him and Meg was too tenuous to allow him to speak freely to her. Instead, he said, "Ah, yes, that famous Sutton temper! Your father was known for his towering rages."

"You knew my father?" Meg asked, surprised.

"Not very well," Wrendale said. "I was a green boy, just out on the Town, and your father and mother were acknowledged leaders of Society. But I can recall the terror that Thomas Sutton inspired in those unwise enough to rouse his ire."

"It is very hard to imagine my papa as a leader of Society," Meg said. "I can remember, when I was very young, he and my mother going to Town for the Season. But by the time I was really old enough to notice, he had already given up all social contacts."

"When your mother died, he turned his face against the world," Wrendale said. "He must have loved her very much."

"Yes, I suppose he must," Meg said doubtfully.

"I was not well acquainted with your father, as I said, but all knew of his deep devotion to his lady. It does not surprise me; your mother was a remarkably beautiful woman." He lifted his quizzing glass and surveyed Meg dispassionately. "You are very like her, you know."

Meg blushed, and an awkward silence fell.

Wrendale picked up the sewing which Meg had placed on a table. "A baby blanket, I see," he said. "I daresay you would not have thought that I would recognize it as such, but there! I am full of surprises. A gift for a friend?"

The colour flooded into Meg's face. "Yes," she said defiantly. "A very good friend, who happens to be the parlour maid at my home. No doubt you think it very common of me, but I care for her, very much."

"Now why would I think it common?" Wrendale asked, eyebrows raised. "Rather, I find it commendable that, despite coming to London, you have not forgotten your old friends at home. You must have a very strange idea of me if you think that I would scorn you for caring about your dependents."

"Well, you told me yourself that you are the rudest man in London," Meg mumbled.

"Ah, but I am only rude when I must be," Wrendale answered. "To depress pretension, or to rescue myself from interminable boredom."

Meg looked at her caller. "You puzzle me, my lord," she said honestly. "You are known everywhere as a stickler for proper deportment, yet at the same time they call you 'the Cynic' and decry your rudeness."

"'Tis not so strange, really," he said. "I believe that to behave properly is to contribute to an orderly and civilized society. This does not, however, compel me to submit myself to the overbearing and the self-important." He chuckled. "In truth, I had no choice but to realize that I was served my just desserts that night at Almack's. You, my dear Miss Sutton, did no more than to repay me with my own coin."

"So I did," Meg said. "But it was still ill-done of me, and I am sorry."

"The incident is forgotten," Wrendale said. "Tell me, shall you be attending Lady Rankin's ball?"

"I was invited," Meg said, "but with all that has happened, I had not thought to attend."

"But you must!" Wrendale said. "Let me give you a bit of advice—when in doubt, lift your chin, square your shoulders and forge on."

"Perhaps I will, then," Meg said.

"And if you will be so kind as to save me the first waltz, I shall be forever in your debt," Wrendale said.

"I think, rather, that I shall be in your debt," Meg said shrewdly. "To be led out by you at the first waltz will be all that is needed to restore my place in society, won't it?"

"Perhaps," Wrendale allowed. "But think of it this way, my dear—it will do the ton good to be caught a little off their guard. Complacency is so very tiresome, is it not?" He bowed over her hand. "Until tomorrow evening, Miss Sutton."

"Good day, my lord," Meg said. She watched him go with the confused feeling that there was more, much more, to Lord Wrendale than met the eye.

In the hall outside the drawing-room, Wrendale found Lady Sally Carstairs lurking in wait.

"Wrendale," she said. "Do step in here for a moment, won't you?" Without waiting for an answer, she seized Wrendale's sleeve and pulled him into what appeared to Wrendale to be the music-room. "Well?" Sally asked anxiously. "Is all well?"

One brow flew up, and Wrendale chuckled. "How very dramatic," he said. "Quite like one of Mrs. Radcliffe's novels."

"Do you read Mrs. Radcliffe, Wrendale?" Sally asked in surprise. "I shouldn't have thought that she would be quite to your taste, being so very Gothic, and with all those dark, fierce-looking men...but what am I saying? Wrendale, how went your interview with Meg? Was she—" she hesitated "—cordial?"

"Very much so," Wrendale said. "A most charming young lady."

"It is good of you to say that," Sally Carstairs said approvingly. "Whatever may be said of you, Wrendale, you are never small, that I must allow. And after the way Meg has treated you! You've been extraordinarily kind, and I shan't forget it."

"Sally," Wrendale said, "you are making far too much of the matter."

"I think not," Sally said. "Your attentions towards Meg will ensure her acceptance by the ton, and I am very conscious of that."

"I fear you overestimate my importance, dear lady," Wrendale said. "I am not Beau Brummell, nodding or denying the socially ambitious. I do not aspire to such lofty heights."

"Your modesty becomes you, but you are a leader, and that is a fact," Sally said firmly. "Meg would have continued a social outcast without your help. By coming here today you have signalled forgiveness of Meg's blunder, thus compelling the ton to do likewise. I am so very grateful, Wrendale; if Meg had been forced to leave London I don't think that I could have borne it. If you knew what her life was like before she came to Town..."

"I believe I have a fair idea," Wrendale said. At Sally's look of surprise, he said, "Knowing of Thomas Sutton's habits, it takes no scholar to deduce that the child must have been as great a recluse, albeit unwillingly, as her father. 'Tis not surprising, really, that she should put a foot wrong; she's never had the chance to learn how to go on in Society."

"Exactly so!" Sally said. "With such an unnatural upbringing, is it any wonder that Meg should make the occasional error? Pray do not mistake me, Wrendale; Meg has been very strictly raised, and very stringently educated. 'Tis just that she has no first-hand knowledge of how the world works. All that she knows is what she's learned from books. Though I must say, Wrendale, it does appear that her father allowed her to read some shockingly unsuitable things."

"Indeed?" Wrendale blandly encouraged her.

"Oh, yes! Political treatise, and women's rights nonsense, and the most amazingly tedious collection of biographies.... I vow to you, I tried to read one and went into a swoon—an actual swoon, Wrendale! 'Tis a wonder that the girl doesn't have a brain fever."

"It would appear," Wrendale said, "that Miss Sutton has depths undreamed of."

"She does," Sally agreed. "Which is why it would be such a particular shame if she weren't allowed to have her Season—her time to be courted and feted."

"She is very important to you, isn't she?" Wrendale asked.

"Her mama was my dearest friend, right until the day she died," Sally told him. "After she was gone, I tried my best to stay close to Meg, but Thomas Sutton totally rejected me. If truth be told, I've always felt that I should have done more, that I should have tried harder."

"Now it is you who is talking fustian," Wrendale said. "You have done everything that is humanly possible to ensure Miss Sutton a wonderful time in London. Need I point out to you how many ladies of our acquaintance would have flatly refused to sponsor a twenty-five-year-old debutante? They would have decreed her to be already on the shelf and washed their hands of her."

"They'd have been fools if they had," Sally said bluntly. "With Meg's fortune, she would need to have one foot in Bedlam before she'd lack for a suitor."

Wrendale laughed. "And they call me a cynic!"

"You can't say it's not true, Wrendale," Sally pointed out. "When Meg mentioned the size of her income and holdings to me, I was quite taken aback. She is an extremely wealthy young woman."

"And thus fair prey to any greedy young lickspittle on the Town," Wrendale remarked. "I don't envy you the role you've taken on, Sally."

"I don't envy it myself," Sally retorted. "But let poor Meg languish in the wilds of the country I will not."

"Well, for whatever meager comfort it is to you, Sally," Wrendale said, making ready to leave, "I'll help in any way I can."

"You will?" Sally Carstairs was stunned. "Wrendale, how can I thank you?"

"Wait and see," Wrendale said, with his hand on the doorknob, "if I can help you or harm you, before you thank me!"

JOHNNY TREVORE WAS strolling along Green Street, swinging his cane and whistling a tune which was all the rage among the young bucks in Town. He doffed his hat and winked at a pretty young serving maid, then bowed deeply to the scandalized dowager whom the maid accompanied. A vendor called out to Johnny, and the young man purchased a posy to tuck in his lapel. When the man cheerfully wished Johnny "a very good day, guv'ner," Johnny tossed him an extra coin and laughed at his comically pleased expression.

A chaise and four pulled up beside Johnny. "Johnny!" Patsy Billington said. "Get in, get in."

"This is something like," Johnny said happily as he climbed into the chaise. "A perfect way to start the day."

Patsy tapped her groom on the shoulder. "Higgins," she said, "Mr. Trevore will drive me home. Pray see yourself back to the house, and do stop on the way for a tankard of ale, if you wish." She pressed a coin into the boy's hand; Johnny settled himself in the groom's place and took up the ribbons.

"Where have you been?" Patsy said, sounding tired and irritable. "I have been looking for you since yesterday morning."

"Oh, here and there," Johnny said blithely. "I was not engaged to see you until this evening, was I?" He stole a look at Patsy's set expression, and his face lit up. "By God," he said, "I can't believe it—you're jealous, aren't you?"

"Don't be a fool, Johnny," Patsy snapped.

Johnny looked crestfallen. "I say, there's no need to be insulting!"

Patsy sighed. She reached out a hand and squeezed Johnny's arm. "I'm sorry," she said softly. "I am feeling a trifle out of curl today, but I shouldn't take it out on you. Forgive me?"

"Of course," Johnny said. He noticed how very pale Patsy was, and the lines furrowed in her forehead. "What's wrong?" he asked sharply. "You do not look well, sweetheart. What is it?"

"I . . . I did not sleep well," Patsy mumbled.

"I know what's troubling you," Johnny exclaimed.

"You do?" Patsy said.

"What an oaf I am not to have realized it immediately," he said. "It's Wrendale, isn't it? He was not very friendly to you when we encountered him at Hyde Park; that's it, I'll wager. He hurt your feelings."

"No, no, not at all," Patsy said impatiently. "Wrendale was quite right to look so disapproving. I should never have gone riding with you at the fashionable hour; too many members of the ton were present. With your mother in Town, I should have been more discreet. I have no doubt that it would distress your mama greatly to have heard you were seen riding with me."

Johnny grinned engagingly. "You needn't worry about my mother," he said. "I've a scheme which will keep her happy while she's in London."

Patsy was not listening. "Johnny," she said abruptly, "what have you done to make Roger Marden angry with you?"

"Roger Marden?" Johnny repeated, puzzled. "Nothing that I know of, but of what moment would it be if I had? I shouldn't care a whit if Marden cordially detested me; he's a wrong 'un, and nothing will convince me otherwise.''

"Oh, Johnny,'' Patsy said. "You mustn't underestimate Marden. He's a dangerous man, and a very bad enemy. Promise me that you will take care. Do you promise?''

"What is this all about, Patsy?'' Johnny asked, frowning. "What has put you in such a taking?''

Patsy pressed a hand to her head. She had thought of nothing else since Marden had left her the day before; the more she had thought on the matter, the more convinced she had become that Johnny was in deadly peril. No one knew better than she the lengths to which Marden would go to attain his goals; the fact that she had no idea what Marden's goal was only made her more uneasy. "Never mind!'' she said faintly. "I only saw Marden looking at you strangely, that day in the Park, and wondered what could be behind it.''

"Goose,'' Johnny said fondly. "However Marden may have looked, you've no cause to be alarmed, I assure you.''

Patsy changed tacks. "Johnny,'' she said, eyes fixed on her clenched hands, "might we go to Paris for a short visit?'' She was convinced that the only way to keep Johnny safe was to remove him from Marden's reach. "It is said to be very beautiful at this time of year.''

Johnny looked thunderstruck. "But, Patsy!'' he exclaimed. "I've asked you to go so many times, and you've always said no.''

Patsy shrugged. "I've changed my mind,'' she said simply. "May we?''

"I'm afraid not, my dear,'' Johnny said gently. "Much as I long to take you, this would be a very poor time for me to leave London. You must see that; with my mother just arrived in Town for the first time in God knows how long, 'twould present too odd an appearance for me to turn round and go away. Perhaps in a few months..."

"I don't want to go in a few months," Patsy said mulishly. "I want to go now."

"I'm sorry, sweeting, but it just isn't possible at this time."

"So much for your declarations of eternal devotion," Patsy said, desperate to goad Johnny into agreeing. "Eternity did not last very long, did it?"

"That's not fair," Johnny protested. He pulled the chaise up before Patsy's home, and turned to his mistress. "Some other time, I'll—"

"Pray banish the notion from your mind," Patsy said stiffly, hopping out of the chaise without waiting to be helped. "'Twas my mistake, to think that all your promises to me meant anything."

"But, Patsy," Johnny protested. "They did!"

Patsy allowed herself to hope. "Will you take me, then?"

"I can't," the young man said. "I just can't!"

"Good day, Mr. Trevore," Patsy Billington said. She strode away, her back to Johnny, afraid that if she looked at him he would see the stark, desperate foreboding which filled her eyes.

CHAPTER SEVEN

MEG SUTTON PAUSED at the entrance to the ball-room. With head held high, her chin raised proudly, she surveyed the elegant assemblage of guests. Her gown, of a deep bronze satin, fell straight from a square neckline, with no ornamentation other than the diamonds that twinkled at her throat and ears. While girls just out did not normally wear anything but the lightest shades, Sally had decreed that, because Meg was a little older than the average debutante, it would be perfectly acceptable for her to be a little more daring in her choice of colours. It was a wise decision; the darker shade made Meg's hair glow as if afire and lent her skin a warm becoming blush.

But it was not the dress alone, nor the excitement of the evening, which had raised the colour in Meg's cheeks. Lady Sally Carstairs saw the angry spark in her charge's eye, and watched the girl anxiously.

"Well!" Meg said. "It appears that Lady Rankin was not expecting us." Thinking back to their arrival, Meg's cheeks burned anew. That Lady Rankin had been shocked to see her and Sally had been apparent; the lady's feeble words of greeting, with a vague allusion to her belief that Meg was ill and so would be unable to attend, had been almost insulting in their insincerity.

"Our esteemed hostess must not have a son of marriageable age," Meg added acerbically, "else she would no doubt have been a little more kind, and a great deal more welcoming!"

"Such impertinence ill becomes you, Margaret Sutton," Sally said sharply. "Tonight of all nights it is imperative that you rise above these petty irritations."

Looking about the crowded room, Meg was forced to acknowledge the truth of Sally's words. Many covert looks were directed at her; curiosity and an avid expectation of trouble were written large on a great number of the faces which Meg saw. Then Lord Wrendale walked up, and the looks became speculative.

"Good evening, Sally," Wrendale said. "Miss Sutton." He bent over Meg's hand. "May I say that you look charming this evening?"

"Thank you, my lord," Meg said stiffly, aware of the sea of eyes watching them. "You are very kind."

"You will have to excuse us, Sally," Wrendale continued. "Miss Sutton has promised me the first waltz of the evening."

"Pray do not feel yourself bound to dance with me, my lord," Meg said, mortified by the surreptitious looks still being directed at her. "I shan't hold you to your promise."

"But I," Wrendale said gently, "shall hold you to yours!" He took Meg's hand firmly in his own, and swept her inexorably out onto the dance floor.

"It was foolish of you, you know," Wrendale said conversationally, "to try to freeze me with a word. People were trying to set me down when you were still in the nursery. With no luck at all, I need hardly add!"

"Are you so impervious to snubs, then?" Meg said, slowly starting to relax.

"Let us just say that my skin is thick enough to deflect all but the sharpest of barbs," Wrendale said.

"I wish that that were true of me," Meg said wistfully.

Wrendale squeezed the hand which lay in his own. "Are the stares of the vulgar disturbing you, child?" he asked. "I should hate to hear you say so; 'tis lowering to think that my arms round you are not enough to make you forget the rest of the world." He said this with such a comical leer that Meg laughed aloud. "But seriously," he said, "you must not allow them to disturb you. They are shallow, empty people with shallow, empty lives. The sensation of the moment is all to them; because they have no resources, spiritual or mental, they rely on gossip and the scandal of the day to lend their lives colour. Really, they are more to be pitied than resented."

Meg blinked. "How very... philosophical of you, my lord," she said. "And so very tolerant, too!"

"Not particularly," Wrendale said. "Oh, in the abstract, I can be forgiving, but right now, for example, I'm tempted to turn my wrath on the crowd, because they have brought that unhappy look into your eyes." Meg blushed, and Wrendale added, "I'm sure I see why Johnny is so besotted with you, my dear. You are so very adorable when you are confused!"

Meg wondered if she should tell Wrendale that the romance between her and Johnny was intended only to fool Lavinia. After all, Wrendale was beginning to seem less the ogre than she had imagined him, and if that were so, she supposed he could be trusted with the truth. But was it her place to tell Wrendale what was, at least in part, Johnny's secret?

"What is it?" Wrendale asked. "You've a pucker between those pretty brows, Miss Sutton, and this is a night for pleasure only. No deep thoughts allowed, if you please."

Meg smiled. "As you say, my lord," she agreed. No, she would not tell him the truth; it was not for her to tell Wrendale that his nephew had been less than truthful with him.

The dance came to an end, and Wrendale bowed before Meg. He did not, however, release her hand. When she looked at him quizzically, he said, "You shan't go free, my dear, until you promise to let me take you in to supper." He leaned towards her and added, "I don't believe that we've confused the gossipmongers quite enough, as yet."

"Very well, my lord," Meg said. "Supper it will be." They smiled at each other.

Johnny Trevore came rushing up, with his mother in tow. After greetings had been exchanged, Johnny swept Meg away to dance, with a warning to Wrendale that "he'd not allow Wren to get the jump on him again, by God!" Wrendale watched the two dance away with an unreadable expression on his face.

"They do make a charming couple, do they not?" Lavinia said complacently, watching them go.

"A charming pair, perhaps, but I doubt very much that they will ever be a couple," Wrendale said.

"Nonsense, Wrendale," Lavinia said. "My Johnny is quite taken with Miss Sutton, I assure you. I should not be surprised if they were betrothed before another month has passed." Wrendale snorted in disbelief. "Yes, yes, you will pretend not to think their courtship real, only to annoy me," Lavinia said. "But I know that you really believe otherwise; else, why would you make such a point of helping Miss Sutton to retain her place in the ton?"

"It was my fault she ever got herself into a coil to begin with," Wrendale growled. "I am just trying to put the matter right."

"Well, whatever your motivation is, I thank you for it," Lavinia said practically. "You have put yourself out to further Johnny's pursuit of the young lady, and I am very aware of your kindness in doing so. Frankly, I had not expected it of you."

"Lavinia, I'll say it again," Wrendale said, exasperated. "You are fair and far off if you think that Johnny will ever wed Miss Sutton."

"Really?" Lavinia cooed. "Then how do you explain that?" She waved her fan in the direction of the dance floor.

The country dance had ended, and Meg, flushed and laughing, curtsied to Johnny. She turned to leave the floor, but Johnny caught her hand and said something to her. Meg laughed, curtsied again, then stepped into Johnny's arms for the waltz which was beginning.

The crowd noticed. If three dances in a row at a public function were tantamount to a proposal of marriage, two in a row indicated, at the very least, a serious interest between a lady and a young gentleman. A buzz of whispered conversation sprang up among the onlookers.

Roger Marden, across the room, also noticed. Though his expression remained fixed in a bland half smile, inwardly he fumed. Johnny Trevore was beginning to remind him of one of those small dogs which ladies sometimes kept, always barking and yapping at one's heels. Something, he thought darkly, must definitely be done about him, and soon! He would not, Marden decided, wait any longer for Patsy Billington to agree to help him; the pressure must be increased in such a way that Patsy would be forced to give in and lend him a hand. If she did not... Marden's lips tightened. She would, he promised himself. One way or another, Patsy Billington would help him, and Johnny Trevore would be dealt with.

Lord Wrendale appeared at Johnny's and Meg's side just as the waltz ended. He scowled playfully at Johnny. "You evil boy," he said. "To monopolize the fair Miss Sutton goes far beyond the bounds of what the ton, and even your loving uncle, will permit. Give way, halfling. Miss Sutton is promised to me for supper."

"Now, Wren," Johnny said with an ingenuous smile. "You wouldn't deny me the pleasure of escorting Meg... Miss Sutton in, would you? You couldn't be so unfeeling."

"But of course I could!" Wrendale retorted, tucking Meg's arm into his own. "You should know me well enough by now, Johnny, to know what infamy I am capable of."

Johnny scowled, aware of Lavinia watching him from across the room. "Seriously, though, Wren, let me take her in," he urged. "After all, it can't matter to you."

"How very ungallant of you, Johnny," Wrendale said. "And it does matter to me. Since you are so very friendly with Miss Sutton, it behooves me to get to know her a little better, don't you agree?" He quirked an eyebrow at his nephew.

Johnny flushed. He had never been comfortable with the notion of keeping Wrendale in the dark about the counterfeit nature of his courtship of Meg; to have his uncle twig him about his feelings for Meg was more than he could stand. "Very well," he mumbled sullenly. "I shall see you later, Miss Sutton."

"You may congratulate yourself upon your conquest of my surly nephew, Miss Sutton," Wrendale said as he escorted Meg into the supper-room. "In truth, I should not have thought it possible that any young lady could penetrate the lad's romantic defenses!"

Meg thought it wisest not to answer. She smiled non-committally, and allowed Wrendale to seat her and prepare a plate for her from the lavish buffet set up along one wall of the room.

"Your feelings for Johnny rather baffle me, though," Wrendale continued when he settled himself across the table from Meg. "Nay, never look at me so!" he added, throwing up a hand. "I shouldn't dream of interfering; I have learned my lesson, I promise you. 'Tis just that I recall once hearing you say that you would never marry, so I think that you can understand my curiosity. What is it about Johnny which made you change your mind?"

Meg sipped slowly at her orgeat to cover her confusion. "When did you hear me say that I didn't wish to marry?" she asked.

"You told me yourself, on the night we met," Wrendale said. "Was it just hyperbole, so to speak? 'Twould be perfectly understandable, under the circumstances."

"I was very angry!" Meg admitted. "Mr. Fortesque was so very... so very..."

"Encroaching? Unbearable?" Wrendale supplied helpfully.

Meg laughed. "Exactly so," she agreed. She looked about the supper-room, determined to change the subject. "How very crowded it is," she remarked weakly.

"Yes, Lady Rankin will be overjoyed," Wrendale said easily. "To have her entertainment declared a sad crush will make her feel the hostess of the Season." He did not press Meg to answer his earlier question.

"Wrendale!" Lavinia stood next to their table, showing all the signs, to her perceptive brother-in-law, of struggling to control an awesome rage. "How naughty it was of you, Wrendale, to steal Miss Sutton away," she said. "You deserve a thundering scold." She smiled tightly.

"Do I indeed, Lavinia?" Behind Lavinia, Johnny stood dejected, his hands thrust into his pockets. He looked at Meg, rolling his eyes; Meg smiled back sympathetically, and Wrendale felt a sudden, irrational twinge of irritation at this sign of intimacy between Meg and Johnny.

"I have a notion," the dowager said. "Why doesn't Johnny take Miss Sutton out to the gardens for a breath of air, while you and I, Wrendale," her eyes glittered, "have a comfortable cose?"

"A trifle heavy-handed, don't you think, Lavinia?" Wrendale murmured provocatively.

Lavinia's bosom swelled with wrath. "Wrendale..." she said in a warning tone.

Roger Marden chose that tense moment to join them. "Good evening," he said smoothly.

Lavinia ignored the newcomer. Johnny frowned, and Wrendale regarded him with one eyebrow raised eloquently. Only Meg seemed glad to see him.

"Good evening, Mr. Marden," she said.

"Good evening, fair one!" he said with a graceful bow. "I've come to claim my dance; I'm sure all the other gentlemen present will agree with me that the Trevores have held you captive for far too long this evening." A charming smile directed at Johnny and Wrendale accompanied his words.

"We Trevores," Wrendale drawled, "have never been overly concerned with the opinions of...shall we say, the hoi polloi?"

A muscle in Marden's cheek twitched, but his smile did not waver. "I'm sure that is so," he agreed. "Your lordship has ever been known as a man who consults none but his own convenience." He turned his attention back to Meg. "Shall we, my dear Miss Sutton?"

Meg jumped to her feet, only too glad to escape Lavinia's blatant matchmaking and Wrendale's cynical regard of Marden. She held out her hand to Wrendale. "Thank you, my lord, for a pleasant supper," she said nervously. "I am glad that we were able to...well, to make a new beginning."

"As am I, my dear," Wrendale said, rising and bowing over her hand.

Marden smiled down at Meg as he led her back into the ballroom. "Having a good time?" he asked.

"Yes," Meg said, somewhat to her own surprise. "Yes, I am. The night got off to rather a difficult start, but it's turned out better than I expected it to." She leaned her head nearer to Marden's. "I must allow, I am glad to be accepted once more by the ton. This is certainly a great deal more enjoyable than sitting at home, listening to Aunt Sally repine.''

"You'll forgive me if I say that almost anything would be more amusing than that!" Marden remarked, and they both laughed. "But you must be truly starved for entertainment to be so pleased by one of Lady Rankin's insipid efforts. Now, if you wished to be royally beguiled, you would attend one of the masquerades at the Pantheon. I assure you, there is nothing in London more droll or engaging than to spend an evening there."

"Well, I shall hope to go, one day," Meg said.

"Perhaps I may escort you," Marden said. "Though I must admit, I go in fear that we'll have no more pleasant outings, now that you are once more the darling of the ton."

Meg did not answer; she wondered uneasily if, in keeping with her plan with Johnny, she should allow herself to be seen abroad with other young gentlemen.

"I see," Marden said, his face set. "I should have known that once you were reconciled with Lord Wrendale you'd no longer have the inclination to stand my friend."

"But how absurd!" Meg said, regretting her momentary ingratitude. After all, had Marden not stood beside her when she was a virtual outcast? "Of course we shall still be friends, and enjoy many more happy times together, I have no doubt. And what has my lord Wrendale to say to the matter?"

"Wrendale would disapprove," Marden said. "You cannot be unaware of how he dislikes me."

"Firstly, Lord Wrendale's feelings for you are no concern of mine," Meg said firmly. "Secondly, I must tell you that he has never so much as mentioned your name to me."

"Oh, he will," Marden said bitterly. "Never doubt it for a moment. And of course you must follow the lead of one of Society's lions." He smiled wistfully. "I suppose I must judge myself lucky to have got to know you while you were . . . at loose ends, shall we say? I daresay his lordship would have prevented even that, if he could."

"I must tell you, Mr. Marden, that Lord Wrendale does not order my life," Meg said hotly. "What I do or whom I see is no business of his."

"I fear that Wrendale does not view the matter in that light," Marden said. "He made perfectly clear, when he warned me to stay away from you."

"He what?" Meg stared stupidly at Marden.

"Oh, yes," he said. "My lord took it upon himself to warn me that he would take it very ill if I pursued my acquaintance with you. Very ill indeed. In fact, he all but threatened to horsewhip me." He regarded the stunned look on Meg's face with a great deal of satisfaction. "Now," Roger Marden said briskly, "shall we have that dance?"

CHAPTER EIGHT

THE BELL ON THE SHOP DOOR rang as Roger Marden closed it behind him. The proprietress, a shrewd Frenchwoman of uncertain years, sized him up with a glance, then hurried over, all smiles.

"Bonjour, monsieur," she purred. "May I be of help to you? You seek a gift for your lady, perhaps?"

"Not precisely," Marden said. "Rather, I seek the lady herself . . . ah, here she is now."

Patsy Billington had stepped out from the back room of the shop, a gown folded over her arm. "It is very pretty, madame," she began, "but I do think that the lace is a bit much. I—" She saw Marden and stopped.

He lifted his quizzing glass. "But the gown is charming!" he said. "You must take it, Patsy. That colour suits you to a shade."

"Roger, what do you want?" Patsy asked curtly.

Marden ignored her. "Pray send the bill for yon gown to me, madame," he said to the shop's owner. "A lady must have her little elegancies, must she not?"

"No!" Patsy interrupted. "I shall pay for my own clothing, thank you."

Marden held out his card. "Here is my address," he said pleasantly. "I compliment you upon your skill, madame. This frock is chic enough to have come from Monsieur Worth himself.''

The Frenchwoman looked back and forth between him and Patsy for a moment, then took Marden's card with a murmured, *"Très bien."*

"Come along, Patsy," Roger Marden said. He crossed the shop, took the new gown from Patsy and handed it to the Frenchwoman. "We shall be late, my dear." He took a firm grip on Patsy's arm and led her, protesting, out the door.

"Late for what, may I ask?" Patsy hissed, unwilling to make a scene in public. "I have no desire to go anywhere with you, Roger."

"We are having nuncheon," Marden said. "At Limmer's Hotel."

Patsy flushed. Limmer's was a haunt of gentlemen addicted to boxing and other blood sports, and as such, was a place that no lady would ordinarily frequent.

Marden noticed her colour. "Offended, my dear?" he asked smoothly. "It does seem a trifle over-sensitive of you, all things considered."

Marden had a cab waiting; he hustled Patsy into it, and, refusing to answer her indignant questions, gave the driver their direction. Before she quite knew what was happening, Patsy was seated across from Marden at a table for two in the dining-room of Limmer's Hotel.

"All right," Patsy said. "We're here. Now will you tell me what it is you want from me?"

Marden snapped his fingers for the waiter. "I took the liberty of ordering ahead," he said. The waiter bustled over with two plates; he set them before Patsy and Marden with a flourish, poured them each a glass of wine, then left.

"The best sirloin in London," Marden remarked. Patsy pushed her plate away with a grimace. "Too red for you, my dear?" asked Marden, slicing his meat. "As you know, I've a fondness for blood-rare meat." He delicately lifted a forkful to his lips.

"What do you want?" Patsy asked again.

Marden took a sip of wine. "I see that young Master Trevore has not left Town," he remarked.

"That is true," Patsy said uneasily. She paused for a moment, then added, too casually, "I did suggest that he and I might visit Paris, but it was not possible. His mother is in London to see him, you must know."

"Was that his excuse?" Marden asked. "Well, no matter."

"I thought you wanted him out of Town?" Patsy asked sharply.

"I've changed my mind," Marden said.

Patsy was relieved, but still suspicious. "I'm glad you've finally banished that maggot from your brain."

"Yes," Marden said imperturbably, "I've come to the conclusion that Johnny's absence from Town is no longer adequate for my purposes." He sliced another bit of sirloin. "I've decided that 'twould be much more the thing if you were to marry him."

Patsy Billington burst out laughing.

Marden's arm snaked across the table and he grabbed Patsy's wrist. "Do not," he said tightly, "push me too far!" The look in his eyes was enough to put an abrupt end to Patsy's laughter.

"But you must see that it is absurd," she said. "Johnny Trevore would never so far forget himself as to offer me marriage. I wouldn't accept him if he did!''

"He would offer," Marden said, "if you threatened to publish his love letters if he did not."

Patsy stared at him, aghast. "If I threatened . . . Never!" she gasped.

"Never is a very long time, my pet," Marden said. "Be careful, lest you find yourself obliged to eat your words."

Patsy started to push away from the table. "I shan't sit here and listen to any more of this nonsense," she said.

Marden shrugged. "You must, of course, please yourself," he said. "But I warn you, 'tis on your own head."

Patsy slowly sat back down. "Why?" she asked. "Why do you hate him so? Why are you willing to go to such lengths . . ." A light dawned in her eyes. "A woman," she said bitterly. "It must be a woman, and a wealthy one at that."

"How very sagacious of you, my love," Marden said, unruffled. "It is indeed a woman, but she is far more than merely wealthy. She is enormously, disgustingly rich."

"Well, however rich she may be, I shan't help you," Patsy said bluntly. "Not at the cost of poor Johnny's future."

"Only think a moment," Marden said. "Think of how long you have been scheming, and saving every penny so that you might . . . retire from the social life, shall we say?" He chuckled at Patsy's expression. "Oh, yes," he said, "I know all about your little plan, and about your investments with Mr. Silas Brown. But if you married young Trevore, you would be assured

of a lifetime of comfort. And I don't think that the lad
would prove to be a difficult mate; I have no doubt
that, with your many charms, you could lead him by
the nose."

"I don't care," Patsy said stubbornly. "I won't do
it."

Marden chewed his last bite of meat, patted his lips
with his serviette, and shrugged. "It is, of course, your
decision to make," he said. He rose from the table and
took up his hat and cane. "But ask yourself this, my
pet—are you really and truly willing to suffer the consequences of your refusal?" With a bow, and a look
which made Patsy's blood run cold, Roger Marden
left her.

LAVINIA TREVORE SAILED into Lady Sally Carstairs's
drawing-room on a cloud of perfume and pale grey
bombazine. "My dear Sally!" she said, holding out
both hands. "It is good of you to see me, and so early
in the day, too." She turned to Meg. "And Miss Sutton—you look delightful this morning, my dear."

Sally greeted her caller with her brightest smile.
"How ridiculous you are, Lavinia, to think that it
would ever be too early for you to call on me, such old
friends as we are." She tucked Lavinia's arm into her
own. "You would be amazed, Meg, if I told you for
how long Lavinia and I have known each other," she
said, escorting her guest to the most comfortable chair
in the room. "Goodness, but it would age us both if I
did tell, wouldn't it, Lavinia?"

"It would," Lavinia agreed, quite ignoring the fact
that although she and Sally had been casual acquaintances for many years, they had never been particular

friends; never, that is, until they scented a possible
match between Meg and Johnny.

"I understand that I am not the only Trevore to in-
vade your drawing-room of late, though," Lavinia
continued, pulling off her gloves. "I daresay that you
have wished my poor Johnny at the devil, Sally, so
often has he come calling."

"Not at all," Sally retorted. "As charming a young
man as he is, I should be quite happy to see him every
day." She slid a sly glance at Meg. "Which is fortunate, as of late, I do!" she admitted.

Meg squirmed uncomfortably in her chair. She
wished with all her heart that it were possible to tell
Sally the truth about the nature of her relationship
with Johnny, but she knew that her chaperon would be
shocked by their pretense of romance, and would refuse to allow Meg to continue the charade.

"So!" Lavinia said brightly. "While we are on the
subject of Johnny, I must tell you, Meg—may I call
you Meg, my dear?—how very taken my son is with
you. I have never seen him quite so gay; never before
has a lady so captivated him. It does a mother's heart
good to know her boy to be contented." She fixed an
inquisitive look on Meg.

"Jo...Mr. Trevore has been very kind," Meg said
uneasily.

"Oh, you needn't scruple to call Johnny by his first
name before me, my dear," Lavinia said. "I know
how very close you two have become." She leaned
forward and took one of Meg's hands in her own. "I
couldn't be happier about it," she said. "If you knew
how I have longed to have a daughter to call my own!"
She sighed theatrically.

Meg was mortified. "Mrs. T-Trevore," she stammered, "it is premature to talk of such things...." She blushed fiercely.

"Your maidenly modesty reflects most favourably on you," Lavinia said, "but we old ladies can see which way the wind is blowing, can't we, Sally?"

Lady Carstairs nodded complacently. To see Meg happily married was her dearest wish, and the thought that Meg might actually marry into such a highborn family filled her with pride.

"For that reason," Lavinia continued, "I shan't scruple to speak honestly with you, my dear. It is possible that you may have heard some talk about my Johnny and a certain woman."

"Lavinia," Sally said in a warning tone.

"No, Sally, I've always held that it's far better to get these things out into the open," Lavinia said briskly. "It wouldn't do for Meg to hear something which might confuse her." She turned her attention back to Meg. "There are times," she said, "when a gentleman may behave in a way which is difficult for a lady to understand."

"At the very least," Sally muttered, recalling a certain unpleasant encounter between herself and the late Lord Carstairs.

Puzzled, Meg looked back and forth between the two older women.

"It is important, though, not to allow these masculine foibles to assume an unnatural importance. Though we must deplore the lack of finer feeling that occasionally leads gentlemen astray, it need have no lasting effect on a lady," Lavinia finished delicately.

"This is, without a doubt, the most shockingly improper conversation that I have ever heard," Sally said gloomily.

"Nonsense, Sally," Lavinia retorted. "If more young ladies were adequately educated about the deplorable way in which gentlemen sometimes behave, there would be a deal less unhappiness in the world."

Meg's furrowed brow cleared. "Oh!" she said. "You mean that Johnny has a mistress." Meg realized, with some amusement, that the pretty lady whom she had seen with Johnny at the Park must have been his *chère amie*.

"Margaret Sutton!" Sally gasped. "What will Lavinia think of you?"

"I admire her plain-speaking," Lavinia said practically. "And it reinforces my belief that you have too much common sense, Meg, not to take the wisest course, which is to ignore the whole matter. Indeed, I scarcely think that there is a lady alive who is not called upon to ignore something in her lifetime."

"I must say, that doesn't seem quite fair," Meg said frankly. "I mean, they wouldn't ignore it if we behaved in such a way, would they?"

"Meg!" Sally wailed.

Lavinia was taken aback, but stuck gamely to her point. "Pray do not misunderstand me, Meg," she said. "When you and Johnny are married—"

"Mrs. Trevore," Meg began uncomfortably.

"When you and Johnny are married," Lavinia repeated, ignoring Meg's interruption, "Johnny will have no mistress. I'll see to that."

"Well, well, well."

The three ladies turned, to find Lord Wrendale leaning against the door jamb, gently swinging his quizzing glass to and fro on its long string. "What have I stumbled upon?" he asked. "It appears that drawing-room conversation has changed dramatically of late."

"Wrendale!" Lady Sally Carstairs leapt to her feet. "Oh, dear...you mustn't think...oh, dear!"

"Wrendale, what are you doing here?" Lavinia snapped.

"Why, paying a polite morning call, of course," Wrendale answered. He moved into the drawing-room, sat down and stretched long legs out towards the fire. Through his quizzing glass he regarded Lavinia and Sally; when he glanced towards Meg, she thought she saw him wink, but couldn't be sure. "Pray do continue, ladies," he said.

"Don't be absurd, Wrendale," Lavinia said. "Sally and I were just sharing a comfortable cose with dear Miss Sutton."

"Indeed," Wrendale drawled. "Why is it that Miss Sutton looks so uncomfortable, then?" He smiled at Meg.

"I know that you won't wish to intrude upon what is a purely feminine conversation, Wrendale," Lavinia said with a frosty smile. "We shall be happy to excuse you."

"But I shouldn't dream of asking to be excused," Wrendale said. "A gentleman is so rarely afforded the opportunity to learn what ladies really think."

"Wrendale!" Lavinia said threateningly.

"Why don't we let Miss Sutton decide?" Wrendale suggested. He looked at Meg, a wicked gleam in his blue eyes. "Well, my dear? Shall I leave you to my estimable sister-in-law and Lady Carstairs?"

"No!" Meg cried, desperate to avoid further interrogation by Johnny's mother. "That is it say, after coming all this way, 'twould be a shame to send my lord home, would it not?" She appealed to Sally, who nodded weakly.

"Yes, Grosvenor Square is all of a mile away," Wrendale murmured. "An exhausting trek for a man of my years."

Lavinia glared at Wrendale for a moment, then rose to her feet. She managed to summon up a smile for Meg. "Your courtesy is a credit to you, my dear," she said. "Would that others were as mannerly!" She could not resist directing a pointed look at Wrendale. "But we shall see each other again very soon, Meg, to continue our conversation. Come along, Sally. You may see me to my carriage." So saying, Lavinia sailed out of the drawing-room, Lady Carstairs in tow.

Upon their exit, Meg let out her breath. "Thank you!" she said fervently.

"Admit it—I am rather handy to have about from time to time," Wrendale said. "Not everyone would have been bold enough to brave Lavinia's wrath, you must allow."

"I certainly shouldn't," Meg admitted. "Goodness, but she is quite…quite redoubtable, isn't she?"

"She is indeed," Wrendale said. "A *femme formidable,* in fact. It sounds much better in French, don't you think?"

"Anything would," Meg said. "It is a beautiful language."

"Do you speak French, Miss Sutton?"

"Only a little bit—*un peu!*" Meg said with a smile. "One of my governesses was teaching me, but—" her

smile faded "— Papa did not care for h
away."

"Would you like it if I were to teach yo
dale asked. "I am thought to have a tolera
accent, I believe; I spend a fair amount of
Paris."

"I should love that," Meg said enthusiastically. "I
envy you your travels; I long to see Paris. In fact, I
plan to. I shall visit all the capitals of the world, and
soon!"

Was she planning a bride trip? Wrendale thought in
dismay. He began to toy with his quizzing glass once
more. "Will Johnny be with you on your travels, I
wonder? I know that he will if Lavinia has anything to
say to the matter!" He fixed Meg with a sober look.
"This is only the beginning, you know," he went on.
"If Johnny continues to woo you, Lavinia is likely to
become more overbearing, rather than less."

Meg began to fiddle with the ribbons of her sea-
green morning frock. "Is she?"

"There is no doubt. Lavinia is sadly unfamiliar with
the concept of discretion." Wrendale watched Meg for
a moment, then added, "Particularly if it appears that
another gentleman might be edging Johnny out—
Roger Marden, for example."

Meg looked up. In her relief at being rescued from
Mrs. Trevore's inquisition, she had quite forgotten
what Marden had told her about Wrendale. "Indeed?" she said.

Wrendale saw his danger. "Of course I would not
presume to offer you advice," he said. "I remember
too well what happened the last time I was so foolish."

"Would you not, my lord? I should have thought, by your actions, that impressing your opinion upon others was your main object in life." Meg's expression was icily disdainful.

"Not 'my lord'!" Wrendale said with a rueful grimace. "I deduce that I have offended you yet again." He spread his arms wide. "Have at me, then!"

Meg thought, not for the first time, how very attractive Wrendale was; the thought made her even more angry. "You shall not charm me, my lord," she said coldly. "You may find it hard to believe, but I am immune to your manifold attractions."

"Now, what bad angel has been whispering in your ear?" Wrendale asked. "Can it be . . . Master Marden?" He saw by Meg's expression that he was right. "Why am I unsurprised?"

"Roger Marden did tell me what had passed between you, as well he should," Meg said. "How did you dare, my lord—you threatened to horsewhip him! How did you dare?"

"I did no such thing—I should never horsewhip such a one as Marden." Wrendale raised his quizzing glass. "I should have my groom do it."

Meg leapt to her feet. "You are contemptible!" she cried. "How can you be so top-lofty? Do you truly think yourself so much better than the common run of man?"

"Not the common run," Wrendale drawled, every bit as angry as Meg. "Just Roger Marden."

"Mr. Marden is my friend," Meg said hotly. "More of a friend, my lord, than you have ever been to anyone in your life, I have no doubt."

"You foolish child, Roger Marden is after one thing and one thing only—your pocket-book. Since he must win you to get your money..." He shrugged.

"I see," Meg said. "It is inconceivable that a gentleman might be drawn to me, and not to my bank balance, I suppose?"

"Let us say that your wealth is a powerful attraction," Wrendale retorted.

"I must point out to you, my lord, that you do not overly flatter your nephew!"

"Johnny has no more interest in your money than I do," Wrendale said flatly. "What he does see in you, however, is a mystery to me!"

"If I told Johnny what you'd said to me today, you would find yourself very much in his black books," Meg said. "I'm not sure but that I should tell him, so that he might see you for what you really are!"

"Tell him with my compliments, madame," Wrendale said. "But doubt not that I shall have a few words to say to him myself."

"He won't listen," Meg said proudly. "Johnny cares for me."

Wrendale stared at Meg coldly. "If I thought there was any chance that Johnny would actually be mad enough to offer you marriage, I'd..."

"You'd what?" Meg taunted him. "There is nothing you could do to stop us. Johnny is of age, and so am I."

"Do not believe that for a moment," Wrendale retorted. "If I chose to, I could put a stop to this ridiculous courtship in a moment."

"Just try, my lord," Meg said spitefully. "And see if you do not catch cold at it!"

"I pity the man that has the schooling of you, my dear," Wrendale said, standing up. "You'll lead him a merry chase, first and last. But I am damned—damned, do you hear me?—if that poor fool will be Johnny."

"It is a wonder to me that you should not positively long to see me wed to Roger Marden, then," Meg said. "It would, after all, save Johnny from falling into my evil clutches!"

"A promise is a promise," Wrendale said obscurely.

"Is that supposed to mean something to me? Or are you so aware of the indefensibility of your position that you fall back on nonsense?" Meg asked scornfully.

"I told Lady Carstairs that I would help watch over you while you were in London," Wrendale retorted. "Much as I might regret that pledge, I shall not go back on my word."

"You promised...!" Meg all but screeched. "Aunt Sally asked you—you!—to help..." Words failed Meg; she was speechless with rage.

"Exactly," Wrendale said. "So, however reluctant I may be, I am bound to save you from the consequences of your folly."

"Do not trouble yourself on my account," Meg said frigidly. "I shall do very well without your assistance."

"Yes, you've managed splendidly so far, haven't you?" Wrendale drawled. "Pray put the idea of marriage out of your mind, Miss Sutton. As little as I intend to allow Johnny to throw away his future by marrying you, even less do I plan on standing by while that cad Marden takes your fortune and ruins your life. However much you may, in fact, deserve it!''

Wrendale slammed out of the drawing-room. Meg stared after him for a moment, breast heaving with anger, then sank slowly into a chair. How did he do it? she wondered. How did Wrendale manage to put her into such a towering rage nearly every time they met?

She loved him. All of a sudden the knowledge was there; Meg realized with horror that of late, her thoughts had turned to Wrendale more and more often. She had been attracted to him from the time they first met, and at some point the attraction had turned to love.

Meg shuddered and put both hands over her face. How had it happened? How had she ever allowed herself to develop feelings for a man who quite clearly despised her? "No!" she said aloud. "I don't care for him. I won't!"

But as Meg sat alone in Sally Carstairs's drawing-room, she had the unhappy feeling that love would go out just as painfully as it had come in.

CHAPTER NINE

LADY SALLY CARSTAIRS set her teacup down with a sigh. "I do wish that you would tell me what is troubling you, Meg," she said. "A trouble shared is a trouble halved, as my dear mama, God rest her soul, always used to say."

"There's nothing wrong," Meg said listlessly. "I am perfectly fine."

"Nonsense, my dear," Sally said. "Only look at you! You are as pale as a wraith, and 'tis quite clear that you got not a wink of sleep last night. What is it, Meg?"

Meg could not deny the truth of Sally's words. She had tried to hide the circles under her eyes with a dusting of bath powder; she had pinched her cheeks until they stung in a vain attempt to raise a little colour, but her mirror had told her that she did, in fact, look like the wraith which Aunt Sally had called her. "I am a little tired," Meg admitted. "I daresay that I have been going it a little too hard of late."

"Well, then, you shall just spend today quietly at home," Sally said firmly. "The rest will do you good, I have no doubt."

"But I am engaged to go to the British Museum with Roger Marden," Meg said. "He'll be here any moment."

"I'll tell him that you are not feeling well," Sally said. "I am sure he'll understand." She hesitated for a moment, then added, "I must admit, Meg, I would be happy to see you spending less time with Mr. Marden. He is personable enough, I'll grant you that, but I cannot think him quite the thing, as you young people say. I have heard—"

"I have no interest," Meg snapped, "in hearing what the gossipmongers have to say about Roger Marden. He has proven himself to be my very good friend."

"I think it admirable that you do not listen to rumour, my pet, but no less a personage than Lord Wrendale himself has hinted to me that the man is not *comme il faut*," Sally said earnestly.

Meg set her teacup down so hard that tea sloshed over the side and spilled onto the table. "Lord Wrendale!" she cried.

All night, as she had tossed and turned, Meg had found it impossible to close her eyes without seeing Wrendale's face before her. However hard she had scolded herself, and told herself not to be ridiculous, the thought of his smile, or the feel of his arms about her as they danced, had brought on a sense of loss which had all but overwhelmed her. She had cried bitter tears into her pillow last night, tears that she had despised herself for shedding. How could she love a man who so clearly hated her?

"I have no interest," Meg continued, struggling to keep her voice under control, "no interest whatsoever in my lord Wrendale's opinion of Mr. Marden."

Sally opened her mouth to speak, then closed it again. After a moment, she ventured cautiously, "Well, what about Johnny Trevore, then? Would he be happy to see you spending so much time with Roger Marden?''

"As I am neither married nor betrothed to Johnny, his opinion is of absolutely no moment," Meg said coldly.

"Oh, but Meg . . . !" Sally began.

Winters entered the breakfast room. "Mr. Marden has arrived, Miss Margaret," he said. "Shall I tell him that you are engaged?''

"No," Meg said, rising so hastily that she almost overturned her chair. "I'll see him." With one last defiant look at Lady Carstairs, she left, and ran up the stairs to the drawing-room.

Roger Marden turned away from the window as Meg entered the room. "Good morning, fair one," he said with a smile. "Are you ready for our outing?''

Meg hesitated. She was, in all honesty, too tired and dispirited to look forward to a day spent tramping through a museum. "Would you think me terribly rude," she said apologetically, "if I asked to postpone our trip? I—I should prefer to remain at home today."

Marden held up a hand. "Say no more," he said. "We can go some other day."

"Thank you," Meg said. "You are very good."

"I'm ashamed to admit it, but I can't say that I was looking forward to examining dusty art treasures on such a glorious morning," Marden admitted wryly. "Call me a philistine if you will!"

Meg made no response. Marden watched her for a moment, then continued, "I've some good news for you, though. Do you remember when I told you about the masquerades at the Pantheon? Well, they will be holding one tomorrow evening. I was hoping that I might escort you."

"Perhaps," Meg said indifferently. "I don't know if we have another engagement."

"Please, Meg," Marden said gently. "Do say yes. I cannot bear to see you so unhappy." Meg's head flew up; Marden continued, "Did you really think that I would not notice? I don't know what, or who, has made you so sad, but I guarantee that a night at the Pantheon will make you forget all your troubles."

Meg managed to summon up a smile. "Perhaps a change is just what I need," she agreed. "Let me ask Aunt Sally...."

Marden's answering smile faded. "She'll never allow it," he said.

"Oh, but I'm sure that she will," Meg said. "Aunt Sally rarely denies me anything—she quite spoils me, in fact."

"You must know that Lady Carstairs disapproves of me," Marden said. "Has she never told you that you would be better off keeping your distance from me?" Meg's expression spoke volumes. "I can see by your face that she has," Marden said bitterly. "This is yet one more bit of meddling, I have no doubt, that may be laid at Lord Wrendale's door."

For the second time that morning, Meg cried, "I have no interest in Wrendale's opinions! I would be very happy to go to the masquerade with you, Mr. Marden—"

"Roger," he prompted her gently.

"Roger," she said with a fleeting smile, "but how may we manage the thing if I don't tell Aunt Sally? Surely it would be the height of impropriety for us to go without a chaperon?"

Marden looked troubled. "I shan't try to bully you," he said. "If you don't trust me enough to be alone with me for a few hours, I shall understand, truly. It is not to be wondered at, I'm sure. With all the vicious gossip about me which has no doubt been poured into your ears..."

"I do trust you," Meg assured him. "But..." she smiled wanly. "You'll think me the veriest coward, I know, but I couldn't bear to...well, to be cast out by the ton yet again."

"You needn't worry about that," Marden lied. "'Twould only be Wrendale and his ilk that would disapprove." In point of fact, the Pantheon, which had once been a favourite haunt of the ton, had become so rowdy and disreputable in recent years that no person of birth would frequent it. To go, and to go alone with a gentleman, would be the death of any young lady's reputation.

"And how would I leave the house, without Aunt Sally knowing?" Meg persisted.

"You surely have another engagement for the evening," Marden pointed out. "Simply tell Lady Carstairs that you have the headache. She may go to the engagement, and you and I shall be gone and back before she returns."

Meg's expression was doubtful. Marden said, "If you'd rather not go, just tell me." His distant expression left no doubt in her mind that he would take a refusal as a personal rebuff.

"I don't know," Meg said. "May I think the matter over? Please?"

"Of course," Roger Marden said. He bowed. "And, whatever you decide, know that I shall stand your friend." *As long,* he thought, *as it takes me to get my hands on your fortune. Then, my fine lady, we shall see who waits for whom!*

LORD WRENDALE RAPPED on the roof of the hackney cab. "Once more round the block, if you please," he called to the jarvey.

"Whatever yer say, guv'nor," the driver answered cheerfully and, with a click of his tongue, set his horse to moving again.

The man must think him mad, Wrendale thought gloomily. Three times the cab had pulled up before Wrendale's destination; three times Wrendale had ordered the cabman to drive on. Wrendale could only hope that no one had noticed his frequent stops before Lady Carstairs's home. If they had, they might well wonder if he were a burglar, studying the house with an eye to breaking in!

Wrendale leaned back against the dusty squabs of the cab. To the devil with the girl! he thought rebelliously. Why should he be obliged to apologize to Meg Sutton? Her behaviour the previous day had been the outside of enough. How she had ever dared to speak to him in the way she had was more than Wrendale could fathom.

Unfortunately, however hard he tried, Wrendale could not stifle the small voice in his head which told him that he was equally to blame. As angry as he was with Miss Sutton, he was, much to his own chagrin, equally appalled by his own reaction to her tirade. He grimaced at the thought of some of the things he had said to her. Anyone listening, he reflected, would have thought he and Meg a pair of particularly strident fishmongers. Thinking back on the argument, Wrendale realized that, however badly Miss Sutton might have behaved, it did not excuse his own incivility.

Once more the hackney cab pulled up before the Carstairs's residence. Wrendale sighed, and reached for the door handle. Before he could open it, a figure crouched in the recessed kitchen entryway of the house across the street caught his eye. What was this?

Willy Fortesque turned up the collar of his coat and stifled a yawn. Unaware that he was being observed, he pulled a flask from his frock-coat pocket and took a deep pull, smacking his lips as he replaced the cork and stowed the bottle back in his pocket.

"What do yer say, guv? Once more about?" the jarvey called down to Wrendale.

"No," Wrendale said softly, never taking his eyes from Fortesque. "Go down the street another house or two, then stop. I've the fancy to sit quietly for a bit."

"All right and tight with me," the jarvey answered, obeying Wrendale's command. "It's yer blunt, it is."

Wrendale settled back in his seat, all the while wondering what in blazes Willy Fortesque was doing. It was clear by the young man's frequent yawns and generally scruffy appearance that he had been in his present location for some time. But to what purpose? Wrendale wondered.

Wrendale's question was answered, at least in part, when the door to Lady Carstairs's house opened and Roger Marden emerged into the sunshine. Marden looked up and down the street, crossed over and stepped into the entryway, where he and Fortesque were soon engulfed in conversation.

The two men conversed for some minutes before Marden handed Fortesque what looked to Wrendale like a roll of money. Then Roger Marden tipped his hat to Fortesque and they separated, walking away from each other until they had both disappeared from view.

Wrendale sat back and stared blindly at the gold-headed cane he carried. Just what, he asked himself, was the meaning of all that? Why would Willy Fortesque be camped on Meg Sutton's doorstep, and why would Roger Marden be giving him money?

"Wren, is that you?" Wrendale was pulled from his brown study by the sound of Johnny Trevore's voice.

Wrendale's nephew stuck his head in the window of the vehicle. "I thought it was you," he said. "What are you doing? Why are you just sitting there?"

"Get in, halfling," Wrendale said. "We need to talk."

Johnny obligingly climbed into the hackney cab. "I never thought to run into you this morning," he said cheerfully. "I was just calling to see if Meg wished to go driving later today. What brought you here?"

"You have to do something about Roger Marden," Wrendale said without preamble. "He's up to something, Johnny; I don't like it."

Johnny Trevore blinked. "What are you talking about, Wren?"

"You must tell Meg Sutton not to have anything more to do with Marden," Wrendale went on. "He's after her money, Johnny, and I'm very much afraid that he doesn't care what he has to do to get it. We can't allow him to ensnare her."

"Unfortunately," Johnny said ruefully, "Meg won't listen to anything I say about Marden. She's a dashed headstrong girl, you know."

"Headstrong be damned!" Wrendale swore. "She's headed for trouble, and you're the only one who can put a stop to it. Lord knows, I've done my best to warn her about Marden, but she just won't listen."

"Well, I suppose I can try," Johnny said doubtfully.

Wrendale gripped the head of his cane, his knuckles white against the gold. "For a man who is supposed to feel so deeply for Miss Sutton, you seem remarkably untroubled by her peril," he said tightly. "One would almost question the level of your regard for her, so uncaring do you appear to be."

"I said that I'd try," Johnny retorted. "And you'll forgive me if I say that the nature of my feelings for Meg are hardly any of your concern."

"If you insist on acting like a fool, Johnny, I must make them my concern," Wrendale said baldly. "If you won't take a step to save her from Marden, I can only conclude that you are not fond enough of Meg to think of marrying her."

Johnny flushed. "My eventual marriage is, once again, none of your concern," he said. "Should I decide to make Meg my bride, you will have to accept it, for there is nothing that you can do to stop it."

"Think again, nephew," Wrendale said softly. "There is a great deal I can, and shall, do to stop you from making the mistake of a lifetime. Oh, she is beautiful, and full of spirit, I'll grant you that; when a man is with Meg Sutton, 'tis easy to fall under her spell, to let her charms blind one to her true nature.

But she is a stubborn, willful hoyden, possessed of the worst temper it has ever been my misfortune to see in a lady. In a word, Johnny, she is more filly than you could ever control. She'd make mincemeat of you, my boy, inside of a fortnight. I'll not allow that to happen."

"You are quite full of what you will and will not allow, aren't you?" Johnny said, white-lipped with anger. He reached for the door handle. "One would almost think, dear uncle, that you wanted Meg Sutton for yourself!" He jumped out of the cab, slamming the door so hard behind him that the vehicle shook.

Lord Wrendale opened his mouth to call out one last, scathing remark; then he closed it again slowly and, sitting alone in the motionless hackney cab, stared at the rapidly disappearing back of his nephew.

PATSY BILLINGTON'S MAID extended a silver tray. "For you, Miss Patsy," she said. "'Twere just delivered."

"Thank you, Dorcas," Patsy said, taking the note which lay on the salver. "That will be all."

After Dorcas had left the room, Patsy curiously turned the note over in her fingers. It was written on heavy white paper of the best quality, in a flowing, distinct script unfamiliar to her. Who could have sent it? she wondered. It wasn't from Johnny Trevore, of a certainty; the multitudes of letters which he had sent her had made Patsy more than familiar with his boyish, somewhat illegible scrawl.

Patsy wondered if the note was from some gentleman desirous of supplanting Johnny. If she was ever to raise the five thousand pounds necessary to start a new life, Patsy knew that she should find a new protector, one older and wealthier than Johnny, from whom she could accept money and expensive gifts with no qualms. But her spirit rebelled; Patsy was tired, tired unto death of her life as a demi-mondaine. She was also genuinely fond of Johnny Trevore, and would hate to hurt him. He was, she knew, already past the worst of his infatuation with her; of late, Patsy had seen less and less of the boy. Given time, the relationship would come to an end naturally, with no hard feelings on either side. It was Patsy's dearest wish to spare her young friend any hurt.

With a sigh, Patsy tore the note open and began to read.

My dearest Patsy,
I am sure, my love, that you have been wondering when next you would have the pleasure of my company. Fear not, little one; I shall see you again very soon. But in the meantime, pray do not be surprised if you should hear from a—how shall I put it? A confederate of mine, you might say. You will not be happy to hear from him, I fear; but remember, my pet, you brought this on yourself!

Think of his visit as a friendly warning. If you continue to be tiresome, I promise you that there will be worse to come! I do hope you will change your mind, and decide to cooperate with the inevitable.

Yours, etc.,
Roger Marden

Patsy crumpled the heavy white paper and threw it into the fire. What could he mean? And who was this mysterious confederate?

As if in answer to her thought, Dorcas re-entered the room. "A Mr. Brown to see you, Miss Patsy," she said. "Shall I show him in?"

Patsy nodded. Surely Mr. Brown couldn't be Marden's heralded confederate?

Mr. Silas Brown entered the room, his spare frame encased in a frock coat of sober cut and excellent material. "Ah, Mrs. Billington," he said. "I hope that I do not inconvenience you?"

"Not at all, Mr. Brown," Patsy said, showing him to a seat. "'Twas good of you to call."

"But you are somewhat surprised to see me, are you not?" Mr. Brown asked.

"Well, I will admit to being a little startled. In all the years we've known each other, I don't believe you've ever before called on me," Patsy admitted. She seated herself beside him on the divan. "What can I do for you, sir?"

"It is, rather, what I can do for you," her caller said seriously. He regarded Patsy for a long moment, then said, "A certain Roger Marden came to call on me yesterday." Mr. Brown was alarmed by the speed with which the colour drained out of Patsy's face. "My dear lady, are you well?" he asked anxiously. "Shall I ring for your maid?"

"No, no," Patsy said. She rose to her feet; Mr. Brown noticed how tightly she clasped her hands. "What . . . what did he want?" she asked faintly.

"Mr. Marden let it be known that he wished for me to sever all connections with you," Mr. Brown said.

"He did?" Patsy looked puzzled.

"He did," Mr. Brown said. "He intimated—in the most delicate way possible!—that if I did not accede to his wishes, he would see to it that my reputation was ruined in the City. He hinted that rumours regarding my theft of my clients' funds would put me out of business, if not in gaol."

"I am so sorry, Mr. Brown," Patsy said miserably. "Never in a thousand years would I have wished to see you involved in such . . . such a sordid situation." She summoned up a weak smile. "And you will never know how much I appreciate your having come here yourself to tell me. I can only thank you for your many kindnesses, and wish you well in the future."

Mr. Brown's thin eyebrows soared upward; he gave a dry chuckle. "You cannot think that I would pay any heed to such an arrant bit of blackmail?"

"But you must!" Patsy said, greatly agitated. "Not for the world would I have any harm come to you, Mr. Brown. You have been very, very good to me over the years, and I shouldn't repay you so shabbily."

"Put your mind at ease, my dear Mrs. Billington," Mr. Brown said. "I have no intention of severing our business connection. You are one of my oldest and most valued clients, I would have you know."

Patsy laughed shakily. "That is very gallant of you," she said, "but I know well that you manage some of the largest fortunes in England."

"Ah, but none of my other accounts bring with them a lady so charming, and so very beautiful," he said.

Patsy paid scant heed to the compliment. "But Roger will ruin you!" she said. "If he spreads those lying rumours—"

"I believe that my reputation, and that of my father before me, will enable me to withstand any unfounded untruths which may fly about. Particularly," he added with a wintry smile, "when those rumours are spread by someone as unreliable as Mr. Marden. You must remember, Mrs. Billington, that I am not without powerful and high-born friends myself."

"How very kind you are, Mr. Brown!" Patsy said, blinking back tears.

"Won't you call me Silas, Mrs. Billington?" Mr. Brown said. "I do feel that Mr. Marden's threats have made us . . . well, kindred spirits, shall we say?"

"Of course, Silas," Patsy said. "I am fully aware of how very much I am indebted to you."

"Nonsense, my dear," the older man said bracingly. "No gentleman would behave otherwise." He paused for a moment, then added, "I am deeply concerned about you, though, I must allow. This Marden must truly hate you to go to such lengths to discommode you."

"He doesn't hate me," Patsy said bleakly, "or at least, not more than he hates everyone! Roger wants a favour from me, a favour which I am loath to grant."

The colour in Mr. Brown's cheeks rose; he looked very angry. "The knave!" he said. "But say the word, dear lady, and I shall see to it that Marden is in a position to hurt no one, much less yourself."

"No!" Patsy cried. "You must promise me that you will not confront him, Mr. . . Silas. You have no idea how very dangerous he can be. No, I fear that this is a matter I must handle myself."

"If that is your wish," Mr. Brown said. He rose to go. "Do take care, Mrs. Billington. I should hate to see anything happen to you."

As Patsy bade him a grateful farewell, Mr. Silas Brown decided that, while he would not break his promise to Patsy Billington by personally calling Roger Marden to task, he would see what a few well-chosen words, spoken in the proper ears, could do. After all, he thought, rumour is a game which two can play!

CHAPTER TEN

MEG SUTTON LET THE lace curtain fall back into place. It was a grey, dismal day; quite in keeping, Meg thought, with her state of mind! A day of reflection and another sleepless night had not brought her any closer to understanding her own emotions, or how she could ever have come to feel the way she did about Wrendale. She had tried to reason with herself, to pretend that that one searing moment of truth when she'd realized that she loved Wrendale had been just an aberration. But Meg was too inherently honest to deny the truth of her feelings. However perverse it might be, it was love which she felt for the haughty lord! Meg wondered if there was a part of her which wanted to be hurt; how else to explain the fact that she had chosen to fall in love with the one man in London whom she knew for a fact to loathe her?

Aunt Sally had spent the previous day exerting all her efforts to convince Meg to tell her what was wrong. She had held to her stricture that Meg should remain at home all day, and had followed her from room to room, trying, by overt means and trickery, to determine what was bothering her charge. Sally had renewed her attempt this morning, but when Meg had still stubbornly refused to admit that anything was amiss, Sally had finally given up in disgust and gone off shopping for the day. Meg was glad; however much she might appreciate Lady Carstairs's care for her, she preferred to be left alone with her pain.

The servants, too, were aware something was troubling their normally cheerful young guest. Winters, the butler, had been too diligent in his attentions at the breakfast table; he had encouraged Meg so unrelentingly to try this dish or that, prepared, he had mendaciously assured her, strictly for her own consumption, that Meg had finally ordered him to leave the room. When he stepped into the drawing-room now, Meg eyed him warily.

"Mr. Trevore to see you, Miss Mar—" he began.

Johnny Trevore burst into the room. "Meg," he said. "Thank God you're at home. I shouldn't have come, but if I don't talk to someone I'll go mad!"

"Johnny, what is it?" Meg asked anxiously. Johnny Trevore was the colour of putty; deep shadows circled his eyes, and his clothing, typically so neat, was pulled about and rumpled.

"It's been like a nightmare, Meg," Johnny said. "I don't know if I'm on my head or my heels!" He sank down onto the davenport and raised a shaking hand to his face.

"That will be all, Winters," Meg said firmly, sending the curious butler on his way. Winters left the drawing-room door carefully ajar as he left; Meg crossed the room and closed it, then turned back to Johnny.

"Of course, it won't do any good to talk," Johnny said. "I might just as well put a period to my existence. 'Twould cause less scandal in the long run, I have no doubt."

"Tell me what's happened," Meg said, truly alarmed by Johnny's appearance and wild talk.

"What's the use?" Johnny said miserably. "There's nothing you can do, and it's far too sordid for your ears, in any case." He made as if to stand up. "I'm sorry that I've disturbed you," he said.

Meg pushed him firmly back into his seat. "If you believe that you are going to come here and frighten me so, Johnny Trevore, and then just leave without telling me what's amiss, then you are very, very wrong. Now tell me what the trouble is, and do it this instant!"

"It's...it's Patsy Billington," Johnny whispered.

"I don't think I know her," Meg said. "Who is she, Johnny?"

He jumped to his feet. "I shouldn't be telling you this," he said. "It isn't proper."

"She must be your mistress," Meg said thoughtfully. "What has she done?"

The knowledge that Meg knew of the existence of his mistress seemed to finally pierce Johnny's defenses. "She's gone mad, Meg," he burst out. "How can I ever tell my mother? It will kill her! I don't know what to do."

"What did Patsy say, Johnny?" Meg asked patiently.

"I never would have believed it if I hadn't heard it with my own ears," Johnny said. "Truth to tell, I still can't believe it."

"Believe what, Johnny?"

"I—I wrote her some letters," Johnny confessed. "Some dashed foolish letters, if you must know. And she said..." He looked sick. "She said that if I don't marry her, she'll publish them!"

"Oh, my," Meg said weakly.

"Exactly," he said. "I have been the worst sort of fool, and now my whole family will pay for it. If I marry her, 'twill cause a scandal the likes of which has not been seen in twenty years. If I don't marry her..." He shuddered.

"What a horrible woman she must be," Meg said, "to do something so absolutely wicked."

"I wouldn't have thought it of her," Johnny said heavily. "She's always been so good to me, so kind and understanding. Oh, she's been behaving a little strangely of late, but this...! What shall I do, Meg? I've been walking the streets ever since she told me, all night, in fact, trying to think of what's best done. What can I do?"

"Go to Wrendale," Meg said firmly. "He can help you, Johnny. He'll know what is the best course to take."

Johnny laughed bitterly. "He is the last person on earth I should go to for assistance," he said. "He already thinks me incapable of managing my own affairs. I can just imagine what he'd have to say to this!"

"If you are in trouble, Wrendale would want you to go to him," Meg said. "I'm sure of it."

"Don't take his part, Meg," Johnny said. "If you knew what he'd said—" He bit off the words and turned away.

"Was it...was it about me?" Meg asked. Johnny would not look at her; Meg added, "You needn't scruple to tell me. I am perfectly aware in what low esteem Lord Wrendale holds me."

"His opinion of me is apparently no higher," Johnny said. "He will not allow me, he says—allow me, if you please!—to make the mistake of a lifetime by marrying such a wilful, headstrong hoyden—" He stopped again. "I'm sorry," he said. "I shouldn't have told you that."

Meg shrugged, trying to hide the pain which made her feel as though her throat had swollen closed. "I know that Wrendale dislikes me," she said, as evenly as she could. "But he would still wish for you to turn to him, Johnny. He will know what is best done."

"No," Johnny said flatly. "I'll think of something to do, without Wrendale's help."

"We'll think of something, you mean," Meg said, covering Johnny's hand with her own.

"You are a better friend than I deserve, Meg," Johnny said, with the first smile she had seen from him that day. "But you mustn't trouble yourself with my problems. I got myself into this coil, and I'll get myself out."

"Nonsense," Meg said. "When I was in trouble, you stood by me, Johnny, and I'll not soon forget that. And after all, are we not both members of the Freedom Club?" She patted Johnny's hand. "Only give me a little time to reflect on the matter. We'll put it right, you and I. On that, you may depend."

PATSY BILLINGTON SAT in her darkened boudoir. The light filtering through the drawn curtains was barely enough to allow Dorcas, her maid, to see Patsy, curled up on the chaise lounge.

"There is someone here to see you, ma'am," Dorcas said.

"I thought I told you that I didn't wish to be disturbed." Patsy's voice was thick, as though, her maid thought, she had been crying.

"I know, Miss Patsy, but..." The servant paused. "It's a young lady. She says she must see you. She says as how it's urgent."

"Who is she?" Patsy asked listlessly.

"She wouldn't give me her name, ma'am. She's dressed to the nines, though."

Patsy slowly dragged herself upright. Could it be another emissary from Marden? she wondered. Her first impulse was to send the girl away, but to what purpose? Marden would only send the chit back, or someone else just as unwelcome. Patsy decided that she might just as well confront her caller and put an end to the matter.

"Very well, Dorcas," Patsy said. "Show the person in."

Dorcas hesitated for a moment, unsure if she should correct her mistress; the young woman waiting to see Patsy was most definitely a lady, if Dorcas knew anything about them.

"I said see her in," Patsy repeated sharply.

Dorcas shrugged and left the room. Patsy slowly rose from her chaise lounge and lit a lamp. From habit, she checked her reflection in the mirror, but with no real interest in what it told her.

Meg Sutton entered the boudoir with her shoulders square and a disdainful expression on her face. "Mrs. Billington?" she said.

"Yes," Patsy answered. She was very pale; Meg thought that she looked as though she had been ill. "Who are you?"

Meg ignored her question. "I've come to speak to you about Johnny Trevore." She did not trouble to hide the contempt in her voice.

Patsy felt sick with anger. "You may tell your master," she said coldly, "that I have done what he forced me to do."

Her master? Meg thought. "Have you?" she asked cautiously.

"Yes, may God forgive me," Patsy said. "I told that poor boy..." Her voice broke, and she turned away from Meg. "I told him that I would publish his letters if he did not marry me." Patsy stood, shoulders bowed, for a long moment. Then she swung round to face Meg again, and Meg stepped back involuntarily, stunned by the rage on Patsy's face. "I don't know what connection you have with this matter, Miss Whoever-you-are, or how you came to throw in your lot with that—that..." She took a deep breath. "But you may be sure of one thing—he will treat you as badly, in the end, as he has poor Johnny and I."

"I see," Meg said slowly. "At least, I don't quite yet, but I am beginning to! Johnny said that he never would have believed it of you." She smiled at Patsy. "It appears that he was right." Meg held out her hand. "I am Meg Sutton," she said. "I am very happy to meet you, Mrs. Billington."

It was Patsy's turn to step back. "Meg Sutton?" she repeated stupidly. This was the heiress of the Season! Patsy thought. This must be the woman that Marden desired, and that he was determined to keep away from Johnny Trevore!

"Yes," Meg said. She pulled off her gloves and sank down into a chair. "I daresay you're wondering why I've come to see you," she said. "Well, it is about Johnny, as I mentioned earlier. You see, he told me what happened between you, and, as I am his very good friend, I thought that I would call on you and see if I might convince you to give up this mad notion of marrying him.'' Her smile faded. ''But I can see that there is more to the matter than I had anticipated.''

''You shouldn't be here, Miss Sutton,'' Patsy said. ''It isn't proper for you to be seen associating with such a one as I.''

''I am beginning to think,'' Meg said warmly, ''that you are exactly the type of person with whom I should most wish to associate.'' At Patsy's puzzled look, she added, ''A kind and caring one, that is to say.''

Patsy laughed, but it was not a happy sound. ''Hardly,'' she said. '''Twould be much nearer the truth to call me selfish and heartless.''

''I don't think so,'' Meg said. ''Someone is forcing you to blackmail Johnny, isn't it so?''

''I've said too much already,'' Patsy whispered. She looked frightened. ''He'd kill me if he knew!''

''No one will kill you,'' Meg said soothingly. ''Only tell me his name, and I'll see to it that—''

''No!'' Patsy interrupted her. ''I won't tell you. You couldn't possibly protect me from him.''

''Surely you overstate the matter?'' Meg asked gently. ''After all, this man, for he is no gentleman, cannot really be so terrible, can he?''

''Would I have done this to Johnny if he weren't?'' Patsy asked bleakly. ''Don't you think that I tried to resist him? But it was no use. He is too wily, and too powerful.''

Meg regarded her thoughtfully for a moment. ''If you won't tell me who, then tell me why,'' she urged. ''Why would anyone want to hurt Johnny Trevore?''

Patsy stared at Meg for a moment. As frightened as she was of Marden, could she allow him to ruin not only Johnny's life, and hers, but this innocent young lady's, too? "Because of you," she said finally.

Meg blinked. "Me?"

"He...he is afraid that Johnny will marry you," Patsy said. "He doesn't wish for that to happen, so he came up with this deranged idea that I should coerce Johnny into marriage."

Meg recoiled as though she had been struck. Wrendale! she thought. He had sworn to put a stop to any marriage between her and Johnny, and he was certainly powerful enough to frighten this poor woman into silence. But did Wrendale really hate Meg so much that he would rather see Johnny wed to his mistress than to her? Thinking back to their last encounter, Meg realized that apparently he did.

Patsy, watching Meg's face, saw her distress. "Listen to me," she said urgently. "This man is ruthless; he will do anything to achieve his ends. I've said more than I should, and if you betray my confidence, he will destroy me. But I could not reconcile it with my conscience if I did not give you one last bit of advice, my dear—be careful. Be very careful, for if he has his way, you will rue the day that you were ever born."

MEG STEPPED OUT OF the carriage which had taken her to Patsy Billington's and back. Lost in a fog of misery, she did not notice the rain pouring down around her, soaking her velvet cloak and causing the feather in her bonnet to droop disconsolately.

That Wrendale would prefer to see his nephew wed to a woman of Patsy Billington's age and experience was astounding; a quiet voice in Meg's head kept repeating that it couldn't be Wrendale who was coercing Patsy into blackmailing Johnny Trevore. But no matter how she tried, Meg could not forget all the harsh things which Wrendale had said to her, and to Johnny about her. Perhaps Wrendale would prefer to see Johnny married to a woman of questionable virtue rather than the "wilful, headstrong hoyden" he had called Meg. She smiled unhappily; as recently as this very morning, she would have thought it impossible for Wrendale to hurt her any more deeply than he already had. How wrong she would have been!

As she let herself into Lady Carstairs's home, Meg wondered dully why Winters had not been by the door to admit her to the house. Standing in the middle of the entrance hall, Meg pulled off her bonnet and struggled to remove her wet cloak.

"And you're quite sure you've no idea where she went?"

"No, my lord, I'm sorry to say that I don't." Winters and Lord Wrendale were deep in conversation as they came down the stairs.

"Meg!" Wrendale said, catching sight of her. "You poor child, you are quite soaked."

Meg could feel the blood rushing into her face. "What are you doing here?"

"I wish to talk to you," Wrendale said. A part of Meg thought how very handsome he looked; from flawlessly fitted frock coat to the glossy shine on his boots, Wrendale was even more immaculately groomed than was his wont.

"No," Meg said flatly. She crossed and flung the front door open. "Good day, my lord."

Wrendale took a step towards her. "Please, Meg," he said quietly. "Just a moment of your time—that's all I ask."

Meg's first impulse was to tell Winters to toss Wrendale out on his ear; the difficulties the elderly butler might have in accomplishing this task did not occur to her. But Meg thought of Johnny, and of Patsy Billington, and of the pain which Wrendale had caused her, and suddenly she was burningly, over-whelmingly angry.

"Very well," she said. "Winters, you may go." The butler needed no second warning; he hastily fled to the back of the house.

"Thank you," Wrendale said. "I appreciate your seeing me, when I know too well that you have every reason to wish me at Jericho."

"At the very least," Meg said, keeping a tight rein on her temper. A gust of wind blew a scattering of rain through the front door, and Meg shivered.

"Let me close that," Wrendale said, starting to-wards the door.

"Leave it!" Meg snapped. "Just say what you came to say."

"Very well," Wrendale said. "I deeply regret the awful things which I said when last we met," he con-tinued, after a pause. "I was very wrong to speak to you in such a shockingly uncivil way. But I am most truly sorry, I promise you. Can you forgive me?"

"When compared to everything else you've done, my lord, your rudeness seems the merest bagatelle," Meg said bitterly.

"You are speaking of my gross interference in your affairs," Wrendale said. "I agree; it was the outside of enough."

Meg stared at him, outraged. "'Outside of enough'?" she repeated. "Never, in all my life, have I heard such nefarious behaviour referred to so mildly."

Wrendale smiled ruefully. "You are not going to make this easy for me, are you?" he asked. "Well, perhaps you shouldn't; I have been incredibly stupid, and almost unbelievably blind." He was silent for a moment, marshalling his thoughts. "Many times," he went on slowly, "you have asked me why I feel this compulsion to interfere in your life, to intrude my opinion where it is not wanted. I said that it was because of my promise to Lady Carstairs, but that was not the truth." He turned, and faced Meg squarely. "I love you, Meg," he said. "I didn't realize it myself until...well, that doesn't matter. I love you, and I want you to be my wife."

When Johnny Trevore had angrily told Wrendale that he acted as though he wanted Meg for himself, Wrendale's first impulse had been to laugh in the boy's face. But not more than a moment had passed before Wrendale had realized, with a dawning sense of wonder, that Johnny was right. He did, he realized, want nothing so much as to spend the rest of his life caring for, arguing with and loving Miss Margaret Sutton.

Meg's mouth fell open. "Is there no limit to your depravity?" she said. "You will truly do anything to keep me from marrying Johnny, won't you?"

"This has nothing to do with Johnny—" Wrendale began.

"Nothing to do with Johnny?" Meg cried. "Do you have any idea of what you've done to him? Do you realize that he sat in this very room and threatened to put a period to his existence? He is mad with shame and worry, and you say that it has nothing to do with him?"

Wrendale bowed his head. "I know that I may cause Johnny some hurt," he said. The knowledge that he had fallen in love with a woman his nephew also cared for filled him with remorse. "But truly, Meg, you two should not suit," he said. "If I thought that you and my nephew could ever be happy together, I should never have spoken. But I know that you couldn't."

Meg's tenuous control over her temper snapped. "Is that how you justify it, my lord? Is that how you excuse the lengths to which you have gone to keep us apart—that Johnny and I should not suit? I should not have thought that any gentleman could be so wicked, so downright cruel, but I should have been wrong."

"Please, Meg," Wrendale said. "Johnny will recover from this disappointment, I promise you. In a year, he will be profoundly grateful that he didn't wed you." Wrendale took Meg's cold hand in his own. "I can make you happy, Meg; at least, I ask for nothing more from life than to try. Won't you let me?"

Meg pulled her hand from Wrendale's, and slapped the peer square across the face. "Does that answer your question, my lord?" she hissed. "If you were the last man in England—the last man on earth!—I should not marry you." She turned and ran up the stairs, leaving Wrendale standing alone, the red imprint of her hand slowly fading from his face.

CHAPTER ELEVEN

ROGER MARDEN SANK INTO the leather wing chair with a sigh of relief, and snapped his fingers at the waiter for a brandy. The chair was tucked into a quiet corner of Marden's club; sheltered as it was by an oaken bookcase and a cluster of dusty potted palms, Marden felt sure that here, at last, he could find the peace and quiet which he so desperately needed.

Marden was not looking well this morning. There were deep lines in his face, and his blond hair was in total disarray. Never before had he left his home looking so very much the worse for wear; his clothing appeared to have been thrown on, as if he'd had no thought but to be dressed quickly.

This had, in fact, been true. Ever since first light this morning, Marden had been, quite literally, besieged by his creditors. Every bootmaker and tailor, every jeweller and hotelkeep to whom he owed any sum, however small, had been on his doorstep at dawn, demanding their money. Even the Frenchwoman from whom he had purchased the gown for Patsy such a short time ago had sent a politely worded missive, informing him that she would be *très obligée* if he would settle his bill with her at his earliest convenience; the word *earliest* had been underlined.

Marden grimaced and took a long swallow of his brandy. Thank God, he thought, that his club dues were up-to-date, else he wouldn't have been safe even here! Marden, as was typical of a gentleman of his class and income, lived largely upon credit. He paid his bills, but at his own convenience; it was generally understood by those businessmen who dealt with the ton that bills would be settled on the next quarter day, at the soonest. Marden had never had a problem with any merchant before; never, that is, until today.

It would be quite impossible, Marden knew, for him to immediately settle every one of the bills which had been pressed upon him that morning with civil demands for immediate payment. Why had his creditors mounted this sudden assault—he could think of no other word—on him? Someone, he thought grimly, had certainly put them up to it! But who?

Marden leaned his head against the back of the chair. The club was very quiet; he could hear two gentlemen talking in the car room across the hall.

"...a positive fortune on the 'Change!'" one of the men was saying enthusiastically. "That Brown is a genius. He's more than doubled my money, and in only a few years."

"Brown, eh?" the other man said. "I've heard good things about him. He handles the Duke of Westing's affairs, I do believe."

"That shows you, doesn't it? And the man gives every client the same service to which he would show His Grace. Why, this very morning I overheard him talking to some shopkeeper whose affairs he handles. He was warning the fellow about Roger Marden—you know Marden, don't you? Blond chap, a member of this very club."

"Do tell!" the second man breathed avidly. Marden held his breath, listening.

"Well, he told this shopkeeper to keep a weather eye on Master Marden. Brown said that the man had best get his money while he had the chance, as Marden is apparently all but run off his legs. 'Tis not surprising; I've heard one or two whispers that he is a little too lucky at cards, if you know what I mean."

"These young men," the second man said disapprovingly.

Marden let out his breath. Brown! he thought bitterly. Almost, he could have laughed aloud—it appeared that the elderly man of business had turned the tables on him, and with a vengeance. Marden's threats to Brown had been purely a bluff; he had hoped that the man would be easily intimidated into refusing to any longer handle Patsy's investments. It seemed, however, that Mr. Silas Brown had more steel in his backbone than was evidenced by his grey hair.

Marden signalled to the waiter to refill his glass. As the servant withdrew, Marden saw Willy Fortesque enter the club and look round searchingly; he raised his hand to catch Fortesque's attention.

"Roger," Fortesque said, "you'll never guess what happened!"

"Softly, Willy, softly," Marden said. "I have good reason to know how well sound carries in these hallowed halls." He motioned his friend into a chair. "What's to do?"

"The damnedest thing," Fortesque said, dropping his voice. "I was watching the Carstairs place, just as you told me to, and I overheard a quarrel between the Sutton chit and Lord Wrendale."

Marden raised one eyebrow. "How, pray tell?" he asked. "You weren't actually in the house, were you?"

"They were talking in the entrance hall, with the front door wide open," Fortesque said. "I vow to you, Marden, 'twas the daftest thing you ever saw—the two of them, standing there quarrelling, with the rain blowing in and the Sutton girl shivering like a blancmange. Can you believe it?"

Marden shrugged. "A vulgar scene, I have no doubt, but not terribly enthralling, in and of itself. What were they arguing about?"

"That's what you'll not credit," Fortesque said triumphantly. "Wrendale asked the girl to marry him!"

Not by the flicker of an eyelash did Marden's expression change; only his hand, which tightened about his glass so that his knuckles showed white, displayed his interest. "Indeed?"

"He did," Fortesque nodded. "But la Sutton read him a rare scold! She told him that she wouldn't marry him if he were the last man in England."

"Did she, now?" Marden emptied his glass in one swallow. It was a deep game, he thought, that my lord Wrendale played! Wrendale wanted the Sutton fortune, that was clear to Marden, but he didn't seem to care if it were he or Johnny Trevore who finally captured it.

"It would have done your heart good to see it," Fortesque said. "She slapped his face so hard that for a moment I thought she'd drawn his cork. Then she stormed up the stairs and left him standing rooted to the spot."

Marden's eyes narrowed. So! he thought, there was passion there, it seemed. Meg had always spoken of Wrendale in a dismissing way, but looking back, it occurred to Marden that perhaps Meg was more interested in Wrendale than even she herself realized.

And if that were the case, would it be long before she changed her mind and accepted the peer's offer of marriage?

And where would that leave Marden? Dunned by his creditors, suspected of being a card sharp, it would not be long before the ton would brand him "not quite the thing," and turn their backs on him forever. Marden was damned if he would let that happen! There was no alternative, he decided. He must marry Meg Sutton, and quickly, before she had the chance to accept Wrendale's proposal. But how to accomplish the thing?

"I wouldn't look to see Miss Sutton at Lady Haversham's rout this evening, if I were you," Fortesque remarked. "She was far too upset to want to spend the evening smiling and making chitter chatter."

This evening—the masquerade! This was the night of the Pantheon masquerade. Slowly, Marden smiled. His original notion had been to take Meg to the Pantheon and to make sure that she was seen there, alone with him. The ensuing scandal would have finished Meg with the ton, scared off any remaining suitors she might have had and left the field clear for Marden. But why not change the plan? He could elope with her this evening, and no one the wiser. The only sticking point would be getting Meg to agree to come; if she were truly as upset as Fortesque had said, she might not be inclined for a night of merriment. It also might be well to think of a way to draw off the hounds, Marden reflected, just in case any pursuit was mounted.

Marden sat in silence for so long that Willy Fortesque began to fidget. "Marden?" he said finally. "Should I go back to watching the girl's house?"

"No," Roger Marden said. "I've several matters for you to attend to, my friend; you're about to have a very busy time of it! But first, tell me..." Marden smiled at Fortesque, a very strange expression on his face. "Are you still taking boxing lessons with Gentleman Jack?"

LORD WRENDALE STEELED himself, then knocked on the door; there was no answer. After a moment he knocked again, more loudly, and called out, "Johnny?" He could hear someone moving about within. There was a crash, a muttered curse, and then the door flew open.

"Good God, Johnny!" Wrendale said involuntarily.

Johnny Trevore stared at his uncle defiantly. He clearly had neither changed his clothes, bathed nor shaved; his hand, still clutching the door, shook visibly, and the blue eyes which met Wrendale's were bloodshot and weary.

"What ho, Uncle?" Johnny said. "Come to gloat over me?"

As Wrendale stepped into Johnny's sitting-room, the smell of brandy assailed him. "Shot in the neck, Johnny?" he asked, with the shadow of a smile.

"And what if I am?" Johnny demanded. "Haven't I good reason?" He dropped into a chair by the hearth. "Well, you were right," he said. "Does that not please you? You said that she'd break my heart, and you were absolutely correct. That must fill you with satisfaction, Uncle."

"Don't say that, Johnny," Wrendale said quietly. "The last thing I ever wanted was to see you hurt, I swear it. You'll never know how sorry I am." How could he not have seen how deeply Johnny cared for Meg Sutton? Wrendale berated himself. He had watched Johnny's courtship of Meg, and somehow he had remained unconvinced. It had not seemed to him that Johnny had the feelings for Meg a man ought to have for his prospective wife. But now, looking at Johnny's miserable expression, Wrendale could not but believe that Johnny did, in truth, love Meg. How could his nephew ever forgive Wrendale for allowing himself to develop feelings for the girl? How could he ever forgive himself?

Johnny dropped his head into his hands. "How did it happen, Wren? How did things get into such a coil?" he asked.

Wrendale felt as though his remorse would choke him. "Ah, lad, I don't know," he said.

"This will kill Mama," Johnny said. "I don't know how I can ever tell her."

Wrendale's mouth twisted. "There's nothing to tell," he said. "As it turns out, the lady won't have me."

Johnny stared at his uncle stupidly. "What?"

Wrendale shrugged. "I did approach her; I'll not lie to you about that. But she wants no part of me." Wrendale was appalled to see Johnny blinking back tears. "No, Johnny, don't!"

"You are the best, the kindest, the most noble..." Johnny swallowed. "To think that you would sacrifice yourself to save me...."

"Don't you want to marry her?" Wrendale asked in amazement.

"Want to marry her? You must be mad," Johnny said. "Want to marry a woman who's no better than a demi-mondaine? Granted, she's been very kind to me, and up until this point, I would have said that I was very fond of her. But now...!" He shuddered.

Wrendale could feel the vein beginning to pulse in his head. "I know that you are very angry with me," he said, struggling to remain calm. "And I don't blame you. I'm sure you think I've served you a backhanded turn. But I will not allow you to speak of her in that way."

"I don't know why you're being so missish all of a sudden," Johnny grumbled. "You said the same things to me yourself about Patsy."

"Patsy?" Wrendale exclaimed. "But..." He stopped, then crossed the room and dropped to one knee beside his nephew. "Johnny," he said, "tell me exactly what is going on, if you please."

"But you already know," Johnny said peevishly.

"I just wish to be sure that I have the facts of the matter straight," Wrendale said.

It was Johnny's turn to shrug. "Patsy Billington is blackmailing me," he said bleakly. "If I don't marry her, she'll publish my billets-doux and ruin me."

Wrendale sat back on his heels. "She will, will she?" he said softly. He stood up. "Go and ring for your man," he told his nephew briskly. "I want you to bathe and shave. Then we'll go to the club and have a bite of dinner."

"I don't want to, Wren," Johnny said. "I want to have another brandy."

"Forget the brandy," Wrendale said. "You and I are going to have dinner, and a little chat. And then—" he smiled coldly "—and then I do believe that I shall pay a call on Mrs. Patsy Billington."

MEG SUTTON PICKED UP a piece of chinoiserie, turned it over in her hands aimlessly, then set it back down on the mantel. She wandered across the drawing-room to the window, peered out briefly into the darkness, then drifted out the drawing-room door and down the hall. She was alone; Sally Carstairs had, at long last agreed to attend Lady Haversham's route without her, after she had assured her a dozen times that yes, she did have the headache, but no, she did not require the services of a doctor. Only after Meg had assured Sally that she would send a footman to Lady Haversham's should she feel the least bit worse had Sally finally, reluctantly, agreed to go.

Meg was glad. She did not think that she could have borne having Lady Carstairs hovering over her solicitously all evening long, while the thought of attending the rout had made her shudder. All those lights, and the music, and hundreds of people whom Meg would have had to smile at, when she wanted nothing so much as to be left alone—it would have been a nightmare. A sound, half laugh, half sob, escaped her. As though, she thought, her life were not already a nightmare!

All day her thoughts had chased one another round her head. A part of her still refused to believe that it could be Wrendale who had put Patsy up to her nefarious scheme; it argued that Wrendale was incapable of such a horrific act. Surely her heart could not be so wayward as to fly to a villain?

But the other, more sensible part of Meg could not but believe in Wrendale's infamy, for who else would

have gone to such lengths to force Johnny into marriage? Wrendale had told Meg himself that he would
see to it that she and Johnny never wed, and he had
left her in no doubt that he would consider almost any
lady to be a better bride for Johnny than herself.

Well, she was glad that she finally knew what was
best done. She would write Wrendale a note, she had
concluded, telling him that she had no intention of
marrying Johnny. That should make it unnecessary
for Wrendale to continue to torment Patsy Billington;
Meg could not doubt but that Patsy had been made
every bit as miserable by Wrendale's plotting as had
she and Johnny. Then, Meg had decided, she would
return to her father's estate, and never come back to
London again.

Meg smiled sadly as she thought of the dreams she'd
had, when she'd been immured on her father's estate,
of what it would be like to live in London. She'd
thought, then, that nothing on earth would ever compel her to return to the country once she was free. How
different, and how very much less pleasant, the real-
ity of Town life had proven to be! She was glad to be
leaving, she told herself; ever since she had arrived
here things had gone amiss. Nothing, Meg thought,
was what it seemed to be, and it was so very difficult
to know whom to trust! Oh, Sally, of course, and dear
Johnny Trevore; Roger Marden, too, had proven
himself to be a true friend. But the vast majority of the
acquaintances she had made in Town were silly, shallow people who lived only for gossip and sensation.

Wandering along the upper halls, Meg heard the
door-knocker sound in the hall below. Winters answered it; Meg heard the murmur of his voice, then
Marden's clear tones, asking if she was at home. Meg

hesitated for a moment, then started resolutely down the stairs. It was only right, she thought, that she should tell Marden herself that she would be leaving London.

"I'm sorry, sir, but Miss Margaret is not receiving visitors this evening," Winters was saying as Meg came round the curve of the staircase.

"That's all right, Winters. I'll see Mr.—" Meg stopped abruptly. "Roger!" she gasped. "My God, what happened to you?"

Roger Marden was conventionally attired, but the impression of neat good grooming ended at his face. One eye was severely blackened; there was a small cut next to his lip, and a matching gash by the unblackened eye.

"Who did this to you?" Meg asked.

"Good evening, Miss Sutton," Marden said. He glanced at Winters. "I hope that I find you well?"

Meg took the hint. "Come into the library," she said to Marden. "That will be all, Winters."

"But Miss Margaret, Lady Carstairs left no orders..." the butler protested.

Meg looked at him. "That will be all, Winters."

Defeated, the butler bowed and left. Meg led Marden into the library, then turned to face him. "What happened?"

Marden shrugged. "My lord Wrendale happened," he said wryly. "He had two of his grooms...attend to me, shall we say?" Marden paused for a moment, then added, "Wrendale watched."

Meg could feel the blood draining from her face. Too well did she remember Wrendale's disdainful comments about having his groom horsewhip Marden. "But why?" she whispered.

"My lord informed me that he had decided—his very word—that he would marry you himself. He said that he wished to obtain your fortune for the Trevore coffers, but doubted Johnny's ability to 'control' you." Marden watched the emotions play across Meg's face. "Wrendale said that I would be wise, in future, to stay as far away from you as is possible."

"I'm sorry," Meg said. "So very sorry!"

"Nonsense," Marden said bracingly. "Don't you think that I am aware of how little to your taste Wrendale's impertinences are? I daresay you'd have slapped his face if you'd heard him."

"You know me very well, Mr. Marden," Meg said wryly.

"Well enough to call you Meg?" Marden asked. "Well enough for you to call me Roger?"

"Of course, Roger," Meg said, with as much of a smile as she could muster.

Marden took Meg's hand. "I know how unhappy Wrendale has made you," he said. "But say the word and I shall call him to task for it." Meg started to speak, and Marden held up a hand. "Oh, I know that I haven't the right to call myself your champion, but I cannot bear to watch idly as Wrendale insults you. Won't you give me the right to make your quarrels my own? Say that you will marry me, Meg!" Marden lifted her chin; his eyes scanned her face watchfully.

Meg was taken aback by Marden's offer, but she needed no time to reflect. "I wish that I might oblige you, Roger," she said quietly, unhappily. "But I cannot. As good a friend as you have been to me, I have not the feelings for you that a lady should have for her husband." No, Meg thought bitterly, those are saved for Wrendale! "In fact—" she turned and took a few steps away from Marden "—I shall be leaving London in a very few days. I—I don't expect to return."

Marden was not surprised by her answer; he was startled, however, to hear of her plan to leave Town, and was glad that he had decided to act immediately.

"I see," Marden said. "I shan't tease you about it, of course. You know that you have my fervent wishes for the happiest of lives. I shall always be your most humble servant, Meg Sutton." He paused. "There is one favour that I should like to ask of you, though."

"Of course," Meg said. She was not so lost in her own pain that she didn't realize the hurt which she must be causing Marden. She was grateful for any chance to make it up to him.

"Come to the Pantheon masquerade tonight," Marden said urgently. "I know that it is a great deal to ask, but let me have this one last evening with you, Meg. To prove to myself, and to Wrendale, that this—" he touched his blackened eye gingerly "—did not change anything between you and me. And you needn't fear that I'll make your night miserable with sighs and longing glances; I promise you, I shan't repine. You will have the gayest of times, my dear." He pinched her chin.

"Oh, but Mr.—Roger," Meg demurred. "A ball? Tonight?"

"Please, Meg? 'Tis not too much to ask, surely."

After all that Roger Marden had done for her, including receiving a savage beating and gracefully accepting a refusal of marriage, could she deny him such a simple request? "Very well," Meg said. "Only give me a few minutes to change, and I'll be right with you."

"Good!" Marden said with a smile. "But do hurry. And you'll need a domino; do you have one?"

"No, but Aunt Sally does. It's quite beautiful, made of deep pink satin," Meg said. "In truth, I should love the chance to wear it, and I know that Aunt Sally wouldn't mind."

"It sounds perfect," Marden said; his smile deepened. "Now hurry along and change, Meg. A wonderful evening awaits us!"

CHAPTER TWELVE

MEG LOOKED ABOUT CURIOUSLY as she and Roger Marden entered the Pantheon. "My," she said weakly. "It is certainly very grand, isn't it?"

It was, indeed. The original structure had burned down some years before; when it was rebuilt by Mr. James Wyatt, no expense had been spared to make it as rich and dazzling as possible. The rectangular ballroom had an ornately painted ceiling, as well as a raised platform for the orchestra. Between Gothic arches, boxes and alcoves lined the room. Crystal chandeliers hung from the ceiling, and every possible surface which could be gilded had been, and with a lavish hand. Compared to the slightly shabby gentility of Almack's Assembly Rooms, Meg thought, the Pantheon was a positive palace!

The ballroom was very crowded. The masqueradegoers were a diverse lot, Meg saw. Some were dressed in full period costumes; the Tudor period seemed popular, with many Elizabeths and an abundance of Cardinal Wolseys in rich scarlet. Many guests wore dominos, long cloaks with hoods cut deep, to hide the face. Still others, mainly ladies, were dressed in normal, if daringly cut, ballgowns. The crowd appeared to be having a riotously good time; the noise level was deafening.

Meg sneaked a glance at Roger Marden as he led her through the crowd, one hand positioned solicitously under her elbow. He looked strange, she thought, not at all like a man who had just been spurned. His eyes were bright with excitement; a tight smile lifted his lips, and his eyes darted about the room as he surveyed the crowd.

Marden led her to a slightly less-populated corner of the room. He did not speak to Meg; he seemed to be watching the entrances, and twice he checked his pocket watch.

"The Pantheon is very... very popular, I can see," Meg said, trying to make conversation. "I must confess, 'tis not at all what I expected!" Privately, Meg was a little taken aback by what she saw around her. It had taken her very little time to realize that it was not just a stickler like Wrendale who might object to the goings-on here; Meg had a good idea that neither Aunt Sally nor Johnny Trevore would be pleased to see her in such surroundings. The general atmosphere of the Pantheon seemed one of dizzy excess; Meg was left speechless by the amount of champagne which those guests in her immediate vicinity were quaffing. Watching the crowd, Meg saw several young bucks eyeing various ladies in a way which would not have been tolerated in any genteel gathering. The ladies, too, seemed to Meg to be not quite what she was accustomed to; a part of her wondered why they did not all freeze to death, so much bare skin did they display!

Some hint of her unease must have communicated itself to her partner, for Roger Marden, still scanning the crowd, absently patted her hand and remarked,

"The Pantheon is a trifle less strict in its entrance requirements than is Almack's."

This seemed to Meg so much of an understatement that she could think of no sensible response.

Of a sudden, Roger Marden seemed to relax; Meg could almost have thought that he sighed in relief. "Enjoying yourself, fair one?" he asked her, his attention fully focused on her for the first time since their arrival.

"Of course I am, Roger," she said dutifully. "It was good of you to bring me."

"Believe me, the pleasure is all mine," Marden said. He laughed.

Meg eyed him uncertainly, then turned to watch the crowd, plying her fan rapidly. "'Tis dreadfully warm in here, is it not?" She reached up. "Certainly too hot for a hood."

Marden grabbed her hand. "No, don't. Leave it up, Meg."

"But it is so very close!"

Marden's amusement seemed to grow. "Try to bear it as best you can. We shan't be here long, little one."

"Oh, do you plan to make an early evening of it?" Meg asked eagerly. "I am glad, I must allow. It is such a crush, and so very noisy! Besides," she added practically, "I shouldn't wish for Aunt Sally to arrive home before me. I did leave her a note, but she would still be terribly worried, I fear."

Marden's head snapped round. "You left her a note?" he asked, all signs of amusement gone. "What did it say?"

"Just—just that we had come here." Meg was uncertain. "I didn't think...that is to say, surely you don't mind?"

Marden stared at her for a moment, eyes narrowed. Then he took her arm in a firm grip and began to pull her across the floor.

"Roger, stop," Meg said. "You're hurting me!"

Marden ignored her. He moved through the crowd unerringly, crossing the room to stand before a row of boxes. In the centre, most prominent box sat Willy Fortesque and a young woman—for by no means could Meg think of her as a lady!—of approximately Meg's height and build. The woman's hair, too, was auburn, though Meg doubted very much that it owed that colour to nature.

Roger Marden did not greet his friend. "There's been a small change of plan," he said without preamble. "She left a note for Sally Carstairs."

Meg was surprised to see Willy Fortesque pale. "P...perhaps we should wait, Roger," he stammered. "Tomorrow...or, better yet, next week—"

Marden's arm shot out; he grabbed Fortesque by the throat and squeezed. Fortesque's face, which had been pale, began to turn an alarming shade of red.

"Do not think to cross me, Willy," Roger Marden said quietly. "'Twould be a most unhealthy decision, I assure you." He released Fortesque.

Meg looked back and forth between Marden and Fortesque. "What is going on here?" she asked, beginning to feel the first twinges of alarm.

Marden's only response was to reach out and snatch the pink domino from Meg's shoulders. Meg gasped in outrage, but Marden ignored her. "Here," he said, tossing the hooded cloak to Fortesque's companion. "Put this on."

"Whatever yer says, ducks," the woman agreed cheerfully. "It'll cost yer extra, though." She removed her own wrap and handed it to Marden.

"Remember, just as we planned it," Marden said to Fortesque. "Do not fail me, Willy."

"I won't, Roger, I promise," Willy Fortesque babbled, rubbing his throat. "Just the way we planned it."

"I demand to know what is going on here," Meg said, trying to keep the fear from her voice. "I don't know what you are about, Roger, but you will forgive me if I say that I am not accustomed to such treatment."

Roger Marden turned towards Meg, and she took an involuntary step backwards, shocked by the malice in his eyes. "You had best become accustomed to it, then," he said icily. "For this, my dear Meg, is just a harbinger of things to come."

Roger Marden took the cloak which Fortesque's companion had given him, wrapped it round Meg, pulled the hood down over her eyes and began to push her towards the door.

PATSY BILLINGTON DID NOT look up as Lord Wrendale entered the room. She was seated before the fire, staring into the flames, a snifter of brandy in her hand.

Wrendale gazed coldly at Johnny's mistress. He waited for her to speak, or to show some sign that she noticed his presence; when she did not, his eyes narrowed. "Mrs. Billington!" he called imperiously.

Patsy did not look up. "What do you want?" she asked listlessly.

"I'm sure that you know exactly why I am here," Wrendale said shortly. He slapped his gloves impatiently against the palm of his hand; he had not removed his many-caped driving coat.

Patsy looked up briefly. Her eyes were sunken and dim, and her complexion was a pasty grey colour; she looked at least fifteen years older than her nearly forty years. "You are doubtless here to snatch up the cudgels in poor Johnny's defence," she said, dropping her gaze back to the fire. "Pray have at it, my lord."

"I will," Wrendale said. "Did you really think that I would allow you to ruin him?"

Patsy shrugged apathetically. She lifted her glass and took a long swallow.

"This pose of indifference will avail you nothing," Wrendale snapped. "We shall come to some agreement tonight, you and I, or I warn you, Mrs. Billington, 'twill go badly for you."

Patsy looked up again. She laughed, a bitter and ugly sound. "Do you know, you are the second person in a very short while to threaten me? I suppose that I should be wary, but the last man did his job a little too well, I fear. You see, I haven't the energy left to be frightened any more."

Wrendale realized that this was not Patsy's first glass of brandy. "The complications of your personal life do not interest me, ma'am."

"Complications," Patsy said. "How very delicate you are, my lord, and how discreet!"

"I want to talk about Johnny," Wrendale said, a little puzzled by Patsy's strange mood.

Patsy's face changed. "Ah, Johnny," she said sadly. "This never should have happened! He would have grown tired of me on his own, you know. We would have parted friends, and I should have felt as though his time with me was something that he would always remember fondly. But now..."

Despite himself, Wrendale was intrigued. "But now?" he prompted.

"Now he will hate me forever," Patsy said; Wrendale winced at the desolation in her voice. "Whatever happens, for the rest of his life Johnny will think of me with loathing."

Wrendale was silent for so long that Patsy's attention wandered back to the fire.

"Someone has put you up to this," Wrendale said, as if to himself. "That is why you are so unhappy, isn't it? Someone has compelled you to blackmail Johnny!"

Patsy only stared into the flames.

"It has to be Marden," Wrendale said slowly. "He must be trying to keep Meg from marrying Johnny, by forcing the boy to marry you instead. That's it, isn't it?" He jerked Patsy out of her seat, his hands on her shoulders. "Tell me, damn it!"

Patsy's eyes were filled with tears. "He said he would destroy me," she whispered. "I did try to resist, but... I didn't want to do it!"

Wrendale's expression softened. "I believe you," he said gently. "I begin to suspect, Mrs. Billington, that you are not at all the villainess which I have always thought you."

"Roger Marden is a terrible man," Patsy said fiercely. "There's nothing he won't do to get what he wants, no device too low for him to employ."

"I don't doubt it," Wrendale said grimly. "But he shan't have Meg. I'll see to that!"

Wrendale was still standing with his hands on Patsy's shoulders when Johnny Trevore stormed into the room, Patsy's maid trailing ineffectually along behind him.

"Wren," Johnny said. He shot one look at Patsy, then ignored her. "Meg's gone."

"What?" Wrendale took a step towards him. "What are you talking about?"

"Lady Carstairs sent for me. She returned early from the Haversham's rout and found a note from Meg, saying that she'd gone to the Pantheon."

"With Marden?" Wrendale asked intently. Johnny nodded. Wrendale swung round to face Patsy. "What is he planning?" he demanded.

"I don't know," Patsy said. "I swear it!"

"Are you part of this, Patsy?" Johnny asked incredulously. "Could you be that wicked? To ruin an innocent girl?"

"No, Johnny, no," Patsy said miserably, holding out a hand. "Please believe me!"

"Be quiet, Johnny," Wrendale said. "Mrs. Billington, you needn't worry any longer. Put your mind at rest; I will deal with Marden." He smiled fleetingly. "You are every bit as kind as Johnny once told me you were, and I am a cad for every thinking otherwise." He bowed over her hand; as he did, he murmured, for Patsy's ears only, "I will see to it that Johnny learns the truth. He will bless your memory, my dear, not hate it!"

"Thank you, my lord," Patsy said, struggling to control her tears. "You are kind indeed."

Patsy's maid stepped into the room once again. "A caller for you, Miss Patsy," she said, eyeing Wrendale and Johnny askance. "Mr. Brown, it is."

"I'm sure that you will excuse us, Mrs. Billington," Wrendale said. "Johnny and I have a call to pay." His eyes glittered. "Friend Marden will be very surprised to see us, I think. And sorry—very, very sorry!"

MEG FELL BACK AGAINST the squabs, panting. "Have you run mad, Roger?"

Roger Marden had wrapped Meg in the borrowed cloak, pinning her arms against her sides, and had sped her out of the Pantheon. By the time she had seriously begun to struggle and cry out for help, they had reached the coach which Marden had apparently had waiting, and Marden had pushed her inside.

He climbed in, shut the door, and settled himself across from her. "Not at all," he said. "It should be clear to you by now exactly what is in my mind, my dear."

Meg tried to pretend that her heart was not hammering against her ribs. "A midnight elopement?" she asked lightly. "Not that hoary old chestnut, surely."

Marden shrugged gracefully. "Sometimes old stories are the best ones."

"But you can't think that you'll get away with it?"

"I have got away with it," Marden said smugly. "Here you are, and we are on our way to Scotland, are we not?"

"Someone will come after me," Meg said bravely. "I did leave a note, if you recall."

Marden chuckled to himself. "So you did," he acknowledged. "Unfortunately for you, I had already made arrangements to have another fox draw the scent, so to speak."

"What are you talking about?" Meg demanded.

"Did you not wonder why Willy Fortesque and his . . . lady friend were present? Didn't it strike you as ino?" Meg looked uncertain; Marden chuckled again. "You see, my dear, while we sit here, all comfortable and cosy, on our way to be wed, Willy and his companion are making a very dramatic—and very obvious—departure from the masquerade. Did you notice that the girl looked somewhat like you? Dressed in your highly visible domino, protesting loudly as Willy forces her to leave with him, can you doubt that she will be the object of all eyes? If any pursuit should be mounted, the pursuers will chase Willy and his friend—who are, of course, headed in an entirely different direction than the one we are taking. So you needn't wait for Wrendale to rescue you, my dear. It shan't happen."

"Why?" Meg whispered. "Why are you doing all this?"

"For your fortune, of course," Marden said matter-of-factly. "The thought that all that lovely, lovely money should go to Johnny Trevore—or, worse yet, Wrendale!—was simply too much to be borne. Oh, I had hoped to marry you in the more conventional way, but circumstances conspired to make that quite impossible. Thus, here we are."

"So your friendship was all a sham," Meg said. "What a fool I have been!"

"Don't feel too badly, my pet," Marden said. "There was never any possibility that you would escape me. I laid my plans too carefully!" He touched the cut by his eye and winced. "Right down to having Willy Fortesque lay ungentle hands on me, to help convince your tender heart that you owed it to me to come to the masquerade this evening."

"However clever you may have been to get me here, your plot will fail," Meg said, with a great deal more conviction than she actually felt. "You may force me to the altar, but you cannot force me to say 'I do.'"

"There are those in Gretna Green," Marden remarked, "who are not overly scrupulous in such matters. We will be wed, with or without your consent."

"Well, what about when we go back to London?" Meg demanded. "You may be sure that I will scream from the rooftops how you have wronged me."

"You may scream," Marden said, "but it won't be in London. No, my dear, I've decided that Town life doesn't suit you. I've a little place in Hereford, very quiet, very secluded; you will stay there, with a couple I've engaged to... watch over you, shall we say? I shall return to Town alone, with the touching story of our romantic elopement. No one will doubt it; you've been seen in my company often enough to lend weight to my tale of runaway love. Oh, Sally Carstairs may not believe it, but she won't dare question it publicly; only think of the scandal!" Marden leaned forward, a smug expression on his face. "Accept it, Meg. I have you and I shall keep you."

Meg was in shock. Back to a life of total seclusion, she thought. Back to the prison which she was so certain she had escaped forever with her father's death. "Wrendale was right about you, right in every particular," she said. "But I was too stubborn and too foolish to listen."

"For which I can only thank you, my dear, from the bottom of my heart," Marden said mockingly. "I must allow, Wrendale was tiresome throughout this little affair. I would bear him great resentment, were it not for the fact that I have so thoroughly beaten him. Come, Meg, you must applaud my generalship! First I lured Johnny Trevore into an ambush—"

"Of course!" Meg gasped. "It was you, wasn't it? You were the one that tormented poor Patsy Billington so badly that she tried to blackmail Johnny."

Marden raised one eyebrow. "But of course," he answered. "A brilliant plan, do you not agree? And it would have worked, too. But imagine my chagrin when I learned that no sooner had I dealt with Johnny than Wrendale himself proposed marriage to you."

"How did you know that?" Meg asked blankly. "I didn't tell anyone!"

Marden shrugged. "I have my ways," he said modestly. "At any event, it was a blow, I won't deny it. But all has come right in the end, hasn't it? I have you, and Wrendale hasn't." Marden chuckled suddenly. "I've just had the most delicious thought," he said. "Perhaps, after you've been in Hereford long enough to become reconciled to your new position, I'll bring you back to London for a time. Wouldn't it be a delight to see the expression on Wrendale's face as I parade into Almack's with you on my arm? I daresay he'd choke on his bile."

"I hate you," Meg cried. "I hate you!"

Roger Marden shifted in his seat, propping his shoulder against the corner of the coach. "That, my dear Meg, is simply the sauce on the goose." With a smile, he closed his eyes and leaned his head back to sleep.

CHAPTER THIRTEEN

LORD WRENDALE and Johnny Trevore paused on the threshold of the Pantheon ballroom. Wrendale's expression hardened as he looked about the room; he could see that, true to its reputation, the masquerade had deteriorated into what could only be called a sad romp. Wrendale could see at least four couples openly kissing, while myriad more flirted brazenly, and danced the waltz in a way which could only be called suggestive.

"Good Lord," Johnny said faintly. "I'd heard that these Pantheon entertainments were not quite the thing, but—"

"Precisely," Wrendale said. He crossed the room, weaving skilfully between the dancers, until he reached a footman standing impassively beneath one of the chandeliers.

"I'm looking for a lady," Wrendale said bluntly. "Perhaps you could help me?"

"Lor' love you, milord, but there do be a mort o' ladies here tonight!" the young servant said with a cocky grin.

Wrendale passed the man a coin, and the footman's expression became suddenly eager. "A particular lady," Wrendale said.

"In a pink domino," Johnny added; Lady Carstairs had mentioned in her note that her domino was missing and Meg was most likely wearing it.

"A pink domino, you says?" the footman said, eyes goggling. "Why didn't you say so? A rare dustup you missed with that little filly—the whole ballroom were a-twitter!"

"What do you mean?" Wrendale's expression was such that the man shrank back.

"Beggin' yer pardon yer lordship, but I meant no disrespeck," the footman whined.

Johnny placed a restraining hand on his uncle's sleeve. "Just tell us what happened, if you please."

"They was settin' in a box, jest over there," the man said confidentially. "Real toffs, they were—you could see that from a mile off. All of a sudden right out o' nowhere, the lady starts ter howlin'. She stands up like she's of a mind ter leave, and the gentleman what's with her grabs her by the arm and pulls her back down. Well, that was all it took ter put that lady in a state! She yells out that this gent is ab—ab..."

"Abducting her?" Wrendale supplied, from between stiff lips.

"That's it!" the man agreed eagerly. "Next thing you knows, the gent's got her by the arms and is pushin' her out the door."

Wrendale's eyes narrowed. "And you did nothing to stop him?"

"Ain't my place ter interfere with the gentry," the footman said sullenly. "A good way ter end up without a position, that is."

Wrendale turned and stalked away from the man. Johnny had seen Wrendale's hands clench into fists; he followed along in silence.

Wrendale left the Pantheon and ran lightly down the steps in front, to where a group of hackney cab drivers stood gossiping. "Ten pounds," Wrendale called out clearly, "to the man who can tell me which way the lady in a pink domino went."

In a moment, Wrendale was surrounded by a half-dozen drivers, all speaking at once. A wizened little man with a battered tam jammed on his head finally won out over the others; he informed Wrendale that they had indeed seen the lady, and that she had been pushed, protesting loudly, into a coach by a gentleman who had then shouted to the driver to "Make for Dover." "Right entertainin', it were," the man finished. "Jest like a raree show."

Wrendale pulled out his notecase and paid the man, then turned and shouted for his curricle. "Luckily, my horses are fresh," he said to Johnny. "I'll leave from here."

"Why Dover?" Johnny asked as he trotted along beside Wrendale. "I mean, I realize that he must be taking her to France, but why? Why not Scotland?"

Wrendale did not appear to be listening. "I can drop you at your rooms on my way out of the city."

"No, you can't," Johnny replied. "I'm going with you. Dash it all, Wren, this is Meg!"

Wrendale seemed disposed to argue, but after a moment, he shrugged. "As you wish," he said tersely.

In a very few minutes, they were on their way. Wrendale stared straight ahead, his eyes on the road; only the muscle which twitched rhythmically along his jaw gave a clue to his feelings. He moved skilfully past slower-moving traffic and, in a surprisingly short time, left London behind them.

"Do you think we'll catch them, Wren?"

"They've only an hour's lead on us." Wrendale was grim. "We'll catch them!"

"And even if we were to be delayed," Johnny reassured himself, "we could come up on them in Dover, couldn't we? I mean, the next packet to Calais doesn't leave until morning, and I shouldn't think that Marden would have the means to hire a private boat, should you?"

"No," Wrendale said thoughtfully. "I shouldn't." He let the horses gradually slow, until the curricle was barely moving.

"Wren, what are you doing?" Johnny demanded.

Wrendale seemed to come to a decision. "Turning round," he said, suiting actions to words. "Stop for a moment and think," he added, forestalling Johnny's protest. "You asked a very good question a short while ago, halfling—why France? Why risk the long ride to Dover, when there's no way to leave for the Continent before morning? Doesn't seem to make much sense, does it? And why that scene at the Pantheon? Marden must have had a hundred better, more private opportunities to abscond with Meg, yet we are to believe that he chose to snatch her out of a public place, and to manhandle her before scores of witnesses. No, Johnny, he is more wily than that. And much more subtle!"

"It does seem deuced odd, now that you mention it," Johnny admitted, "but I don't quite see—"

"I think," Wrendale said slowly, "that Roger Marden has laid his plans very carefully. We have seen, or, rather, heard, exactly what he wished us to hear. And we have done precisely what he expected us to do— hare off to the coast without question."

"But we must be following someone," Johnny pointed out. "There can't be two ladies in pink dominos, both being kidnapped on the same night."

"But there can, Johnny," Wrendale said. "There are! If we followed that coach to Dover, I'd wager that we would find Willy Fortesque and some unknown female in it, loudly protesting their innocence."

"So they are decoys," Johnny breathed. "And, in the meantime, poor Meg..."

"Yes," Wrendale said; his tone was icily calm. "He has much to answer for, our Mr. Marden."

Johnny slid a glance at his uncle's set profile. "Wren? I've been thinking..."

"Yes?"

"This afternoon, when you called on me, you said...that is, did I misunderstand you? Did you propose marriage to Meg?"

"Yes." Wrendale never took his eyes from the road. "I offered, she refused."

"I'm sorry, Wren," Johnny said gently.

"'Tis I who should apologize—I never should have asked Meg to be my wife, knowing how you felt about her," Wrendale said. "I know that it will sound mad, but I thought that you did not really love her, Johnny. I'm sorry; I was wrong."

Johnny struggled with himself for a moment, then blurted out, "No! You weren't wrong. Meg and I...well, Meg agreed to pretend...dash it all, Wren, it was just a charade, to keep my mother happy." Johnny was shamefaced. "I wanted to tell you, but for some reason Meg insisted that I keep it to myself."

Wrendale turned and looked at his nephew. "Did she now?" he asked. "I wonder why?"

Johnny shrugged. "I haven't the vaguest notion," he admitted. "But every time I suggested that we should let you in on the secret, she'd fly up into the boughs and read me a scold. Well, you can see why I soon dropped the subject. Meg is the dearest thing in nature, you understand, but she does have the most ferocious temper!"

For the first time since they'd left Patsy Billington's, Wrendale laughed. "I know it too well," he said. "She is the most hot-headed, wilful, adorable creature...!"

Johnny stared at his uncle, eyes wide. "You do love her, don't you?" he asked.

"I do, indeed," Wrendale said. He shook up the horses, and fixed an unwavering gaze back on the road. "It may be that Meg will never be mine; I can accept that if I must. But I promise you, halfling—she will never, ever be Marden's!"

ROGER MARDEN LED MEG into the inn, his hand clamped uncomfortably round her upper arm. "Now, don't be foolish, my dear," he murmured as the door to the small, disreputable establishment swung shut behind them. "We'll have something to eat and drink and be on our way. No histrionics, if you please." He accompanied his words with a cruel squeeze which would leave Meg bruised.

A woman hurried out from the kitchen, wiping her hands on a greasy apron. Her eyes lit up at the sight of Meg and Marden; it was clear that she did not often serve the carriage trade. "Good evenin', your lordship," she simpered, bobbing clumsily. "And what may I do for you this fine night?"

"Good evening," Marden said pleasantly. "My wife and I should like some supper, please." Meg had stiffened at the word *wife*; Marden squeezed her arm again, and she winced.

"Right away, your lordship. May I prepare a bed-chamber for you and your lady?" she asked hopefully. "'Tis grown late, and the roads hereabouts be powerful bad, with only the moon to guide you."

"I don't know—what do you think, my pet?" Marden asked Meg with a mocking smile. "Shall we break our journey? I'm sure that our good hostess here could make us very cosy."

"I could indeed," the woman said eagerly. "It's a right comfortable room, your lordship, once I put clean linens on the bed and run a dustcloth round."

Meg glared at Marden impotently. "I think not," she said tightly.

"You're quite right, of course, my dear," Marden said. He turned back to the innkeeper. "Sadly, we are obliged to be in Scotland before morning," he told her. "Just a light supper, I think, and perhaps a bottle of brandy, if you have it."

The woman nodded, disappointed. "We do," she said. "If you'll just step into the taproom...? We haven't a private parlour, I'm afeared, but there's no one about in there, so you won't be disturbed."

"Good," Marden said. "My bride and I are still newly wed enough to desire our privacy. Aren't we, my sweet?"

They entered the low-ceilinged taproom, and Marden stripped off his greatcoat and dropped it on a chair by the door. Meg made her way to the corner of the room farthest from Marden and sat down, the borrowed cloak folded about her. She studiously ignored her abductor.

"Pray do not sulk, Meg," Marden said. "It does not become you, and has absolutely no effect on me." He took out his handkerchief and swiped at the table before him with a grimace. "Not exactly the Clarendon, I fear," he said. "Still, she will serve us supper, and I suppose at this hour we can expect no more."

"I should think that you'd be perfectly comfortable here," Meg said spitefully. "Such squalor seems your natural habitat."

"Still so defiant!" Marden said. "One would think that you would devote yourself to cultivating my kindness, under the circumstances."

The landlady hurried into the taproom with a heavily laden tray. "Here you are, your lordship," she said. "The pigeon pie is fresh, and I gave you the bottle of brandy wot my gran'fer brought back from Spain." She bustled about the table, laying two places and disposing the food. "Beggin' your pardon, your lordship, but I went ahead and prepared that bedchamber. Who knows?" she added slyly. "You and your lady might change your minds about stayin' after you've had some of my good vittles and a glass or two of brandy!" She winked broadly.

Marden laughed. "Perhaps we might," he agreed. She bobbed a curtsy, and left the taproom.

"Come, Meg," Marden said. "It smells very good, I must allow." Meg did not move; Marden shrugged. "As you wish," he said, and gingerly tasted the pie. "Delicious! The woman may be a slattern, but she certainly knows how to cook. Are you quite sure you won't change your mind?" When Meg did not answer him, he shrugged again, and applied himself to his supper.

As Marden ate, Meg surreptitiously looked about the room. Was there nothing which she could use as a weapon? There were fireplace tools, but Marden sat directly before the hearth; she would not be able to reach them before he stopped her. The woman had set knives at the table, but Meg could see from where she was that the cutlery was old and battered; she doubted if one of the knifes would be sharp enough to frighten Marden into releasing her. It would have to be when they left, then, Meg decided; she would tell the landlady that she was being abducted, and hope that the woman would help her!

Marden made a leisurely meal, then poured himself a second brandy and stretched his legs out towards the fire. "If nothing else, you should have a glass of this brandy," he told Meg. "'Tis remarkably fine."

"Enjoy it," Meg said defiantly. "Linger over it, as a matter of fact. For every moment that you waste here, I am that much closer to being free."

"You are an optimist, aren't you?" Marden was amused. "Do you truly think that Wrendale will come riding out of the night to save you? For myself, I don't believe that it is very likely. Even if he knew where you were—and I can assure you, he does not!—are you quite sure he would care? From what I have been told, you refused his offer most emphatically." He chuckled.

Meg stared at her hands, clenching and unclenching them in her lap.

"Don't feel too badly, my dear," Marden said, suddenly brisk. He set down his glass and stood up. "Whether you refused Wrendale's offer or accepted it would have made no difference; I should still have had you. You will find, when you know me better, that it is not in my nature to accept defeat.''

"Is it not?'' The quiet voice made Marden spin round.

"Wrendale?'' Meg breathed. She flew across the room.

Lord Wrendale stepped into the taproom, Johnny Trevore behind him. "I suspect that you are about to learn what it is to be vanquished,'' Wrendale said. "In point of fact, I promise it!''

Marden dove for his greatcoat, but Wrendale was faster; he snatched up the garment and searched through the pockets. "Is this what you were looking for?'' Wrendale held up a small, lethal-looking pistol. "I think I'll keep it, if you don't mind.''

"Not at all,'' Marden said, aplomb restored. "Friends should be willing to share, don't you think?''

Wrendale permitted himself one searching look at Meg's face. "Meg? Are you all right?'' he asked gently.

Meg nodded, never taking her eyes from Wrendale's face. "I'm fine.''

Wrendale's attention was once more fixed on Marden. "You've led us a merry chase, Master Marden,'' he said. "It served for naught, though. Here we are!''

"I shouldn't say that it was totally wasted, myself,'' Marden responded. "Should you, sweeting?'' He smiled at Meg.

"Don't call me that!'' Meg cried.

"Second thoughts, my love?'' Marden said, one eyebrow raised. "You mustn't let Wrendale's presence inhibit you; our elopement is none of his concern.''

"Elopement?" Meg sputtered. "It was no such thing—you forced me to come!"

"I am hurt, truly," Marden said, openly mocking. "After all that we have been to each other..."

"You have been nothing to me but trouble," Meg said. "And I have been nothing but a fool!" She looked at Wrendale, her heart in her eyes.

"Don't distress yourself, love," Wrendale said quietly. "All will be well now."

"I'm not sure that you'll think so, actually," Marden remarked. He sat back down at the table and casually crossed his legs. "Things have gone rather too far between Meg and me for you to interfere, my lord. Shall I elaborate?"

Wrendale did not look away from Marden. "Johnny," he said, "take Meg and my curricle and go back to London. I'll find my own way home."

Johnny looked back and forth between Marden, who had a satisfied smile on his face, and his uncle, whose fingers clenched the pistol so tightly that his knuckles showed white. "I don't think that I should leave, Wren," he said worriedly.

"Indeed you shouldn't, Johnny," Marden agreed. "Wrendale will need you to drive him home. Meg and I are going on to Scotland, and I don't believe that you will wish to stop us."

"Shall I not?" Wrendale asked softly.

"Not unless you wish to see Meg's reputation destroyed." Marden was triumphant. "You see, while you were chasing round the countryside tonight, Meg and I were making good use of the bedchamber upstairs."

"You lie!" Meg would have flown at Marden, had Johnny not put out a hand to stop her.

Marden chuckled. "Ah, but there's the beauty of the thing—it doesn't matter! The truth of a proposition is less important than its dissemination. In other words, dear Meg, people are always willing to believe a sordid story, if only you tell it to enough of them." He appeared to be enjoying himself immensely. "Picture it, if you will—I go back to Town and drop a word here, an interference there. People start to whisper, then to talk, and before you know it, Meg Sutton is thought to be no better than she should be and a jade besides. Imagine the scandal! Imagine the delight that those less fortunate than Meg would take in her downfall. A sobering prospect, is it not, my lord?" Marden's eyes glittered as he stared at Wrendale. "I vow, I'd almost be willing to lose her fortune, to see the woman you fancy branded as a demi mondaine!"

"You'll never spread such a damnable lie," Wrendale said flatly. "I'll see you in hell first!" Reflexively, he raised the pistol.

"Wren no!" Johnny grabbed his uncle's arm; the gun went off, and Johnny slumped over.

"Johnny!" Wrendale's cry was an anguished wail. He bent over his nephew.

Roger Marden saw his chance. He leapt over Wrendale and Johnny, grabbed Meg by the wrist, and pulled her out of the taproom.

"Go after them, Wren," Johnny gasped. His hand was clamped to his leg; blood oozed slowly from between his fingers. "I'm fine, damn it—it's just a scratch. Go!"

Wrendale quickly assured himself that Johnny's wound was not serious, then he squeezed his nephew's shoulder. "I'll be back very soon," he promised grimly.

"Don't kill him, Wren," Johnny said intently. "Don't let him make you a murderer." Wrendale nodded.

He ran out of the taproom and past the astonished innkeeper, her mouth agape. "See to my nephew!" he called and sprinted outside, just in time to see his own curricle tear off, with Meg and Marden aboard.

The doors of the small stable attached to the inn were open, the stalls within empty. The only vehicle in sight was Marden's coach; the coachman was nowhere to be seen.

With three quick strides, Wrendale was across the yard. He began to unharness the coach horses, cursing under his breath. He fumbled with the leather straps and buckles; finally, with an impatient kick, he knocked the wooden guard free, jerked the reins down and leapt onto one of the horses. Still locked in tandem, the two horses bolted from between the poles.

Panicked, goaded by a rider that kicked them both indiscriminately, the coach horses raced down the deserted road. Wrendale prayed that neither of them would break a leg; Marden had left the turnpike to find an inn suitably deserted, and the lane he had taken was rutted and hard. Wrendale gathered the reins more tightly in his hands and urged the horses to greater speed, thankful that at least the moon was bright enough to light their way.

Despite the bad road, it was not long before the curricle came into sight. It was swaying wildly from side to side as it rocked along; Marden was standing, whipping the horses to greater and greater speed. Wrendale could see Meg clinging to the sides of the vehicle, desperately trying to keep her seat.

"Fool!" Wrendale muttered. "Slow down, slow down!" He crouched low; his two horses, running perfectly in stride, began to gain on the fleeing curricle. Marden, glancing back over his shoulder, saw Wrendale advancing and redoubled his efforts with the whip. They were approaching a spot where the road widened, then narrowed as it dipped down between the banks of two fields; Wrendale's blood ran cold when he thought of the vehicle carrying Meg trying to pass through the bottleneck at such a rate of speed.

Wrendale pulled closer and closer. He manoeuvred his team to Meg's side of the curricle, and, hanging dangerously far over, held out his arm to Meg. "Jump, Meg," he shouted above the thunder of the horses' hooves and the protesting groans of the curricle wheels. "Grab hold!"

Meg did not hesitate. She rose to her feet, clutched Wrendale's arm and launched herself into the air. With one desperate heave, Wrendale had her out of the curricle and pulled onto his horse. He began to haul back on the reins with all his strength, and the panting beasts slowed, then stopped.

Marden saw too late that his victim was escaping him; he lunged across the seat, trying to snag Meg's ankle, but missed.

"Watch out!" Wrendale shouted hoarsely, but to no avail. Marden had taken his eyes off the road just as the curricle reached the dip; the vehicle swerved a little when he grabbed for Meg, and one of the wheels hit the bank. Marden had time for no more than a muffled cry before the curricle rode half-way up the bank and flipped. The curricle's horses screamed as the vehicle tumbled over and over. Finally, with a crash of splintering wood, the mangled vehicle came to rest on the road before Meg and Wrendale.

CHAPTER FOURTEEN

"MEG?" Lady Sally Carstairs swung the drawing-room door open. "Are you in there?"

"Yes, Aunt Sally." The room was dim; the curtains had not been drawn and the fire was unlit.

"My dear, what are you doing out of bed?" Sally scolded. She bustled into the room and threw the curtains wide. "You should be resting today."

Meg was very pale. "I couldn't sleep," she said. "Every time I closed my eyes, I saw Marden's body stretched out in the road." She shuddered.

"Oh, my poor thing," Sally said. She knelt before Meg's chair and took the girl's hands in her own. "You've had a terrible time of it, my pet, but it's over now. That awful man will never hurt you, or anyone else, ever again. Isn't it better that way, really?"

"He was a monster," Meg acknowledged. "But to die so young, and in such a way...! I can't seem to grasp it all."

"The best thing that you can do is to try to put it out of your mind," Sally said practically. "Least said, soonest mended, you know."

"That's what Wrendale told me," Meg replied in a low voice.

Sally slid a look at her charge. "What else did Wrendale say?" she asked casually.

"Not a great deal," Meg answered. "First he had to make sure that...well, that there was nothing more to be done for Marden. Then we raced back to the inn to check on Johnny. Luckily, the landlady had had the good sense to send for a doctor. While we were waiting for the doctor to finish his examination, Wrendale sent the landlady's son to the nearest posting house to hire a conveyance to see me home. I waited only to hear that the doctor thought Johnny would be fine before returning to the City."

"I see," Sally said non-committally.

"Have you arranged for a coach for tomorrow, Aunt Sally?" Meg asked.

"No, I have not," Sally retorted. "And I don't plan to! This notion of yours is quite ridiculous, Meg, and I won't allow—"

"I shall travel post if I have to," Meg said firmly. "Whether you hire the coach or not, I am leaving London in the morning."

"Oh, but Meg!" Sally seemed on the verge of tears. "Back to that awful house, and all by yourself! I can't bear it! At least let me come with you."

"No," Meg said. "I thank you for the offer, but you would be thoroughly miserable in the country. It's better this way, Aunt, really. I'm tired; I wish for nothing more than to rest and to be alone."

Sally seemed inclined to argue, but she was interrupted by Winters, the butler.

"A caller for Miss Margaret," he said.

Sally began to shake her head. "I don't think—"

"It's Mr. Trevore, my lady," the butler added delicately.

Meg jumped to her feet. "Johnny?"

Johnny Trevore came into the room, leaning heavily on a Malacca cane; he seemed otherwise none the worse for wear. "'Morning, all," he said cheerfully.

Meg flew across the room and almost knocked the youth over with the enthusiasm of her greeting. "Johnny, Johnny, I'm so glad to see you! But shouldn't you still be abed? The doctor said—"

"The doctor," Johnny retorted, "is an old woman! I told you last night, it's only a fleabite." He firmly removed Meg's arms from round his neck. "Give over, Meg, do! I'm not on my deathbed yet."

"And glad I am to hear it," Meg said, blinking back tears. "Though it's no thanks to me! How can I ever tell you how grateful I am?"

"Don't be a goose," Johnny said dampingly. "What are friends for? At any rate, it isn't me you should be thanking, it's Wren. He was the one who caught on that we were following the wrong coach. If it had been up to me, Wren and I would be half-way to Paris by now."

Meg was spared the necessity of answering by Winter's timely entrance. The butler's expression was pained. "A Mrs. Billington has called, my lady," he said.

Sally bounced up out of her seat. "That woman, in my house?" She was outraged. "I'll not have it! Tell her—"

"Show her in, please, Winters," Meg said quietly.

"Meg, really...!" Sally began.

"Please, Aunt Sally," Meg said. "I should like to say goodbye to her."

Puzzled, Johnny Trevore opened his mouth to speak; Sally caught his eye and shook her head.

"Please, Aunt?"

"Very well," Sally said grudgingly. "Winters, show Mrs. Billington in."

Patsy Billington entered the drawing-room with head held high. She crossed to stand before Sally. "You are very good to allow me to call, Lady Carstairs," she said, with a calm dignity which made Sally's frozen expression thaw a trifle. "I shall not trespass upon your hospitality for long, I promise. I only wished to assure myself that Miss Sutton was truly safe."

"I am," Meg said, smiling and holding out her hands to Patsy. "And I understand that you are one of those I have to thank for it. Wrendale said..." Meg's smile slipped a little, but she continued gamely, "He said that he never would have found me so quickly, had you not made him see how devious Marden is...was."

Patsy bowed her head. "Don't thank me! Had I told you at the very start that Marden was threatening me, you would never have been in such danger."

"My predicament was purely my own doing," Meg said bleakly. "Many people tried to warn me about Marden, but I was too stubborn to listen." She turned away.

"Patsy?" Johnny Trevore said softly.

Patsy's eyes filled with tears as she faced Johnny. "Oh, Johnny..." she whispered.

"Dash it all, Patsy, don't cry. I know it wasn't your fault—Wrendale told me the whole wretched tale. And if you ask me, Marden deserved his fate just as much for what he did to you as for trying to force Meg to the altar!"

"Thank you, my dear," Patsy said softly. "You are very good." Patsy looked round the room as she drew on her gloves. "I've also come to say goodbye," she told them. "I shall be leaving London tomorrow, and I shan't return."

"But where are you going?" Johnny demanded. "This isn't necessary, you know. I'm willing to continue—"

"But I am not, Johnny," Patsy said lightly. "I am leaving London with my husband, you see. I was married by special licence, this morning."

Johnny gaped at her. "To whom?"

"Mr. Silas Brown," Patsy said.

"Congratulations," Meg said warmly. "I don't know this Mr. Brown, but I wish you both very happy."

"The man is an octogenarian," Johnny burst out. "Dash it all, Patsy, you can't marry him—he's old enough to be your grandfather!"

"My father, perhaps," Patsy corrected him gently. "You forget, Johnny, I am very much older than you! And I do believe that we shall be happy—at least, Silas believes so, and he has gone a long way towards convincing me. And you mustn't think that I am taking advantage of him, either," she added. "Silas knows what my style of life has been. He doesn't mind."

"Are you sure, Patsy?" Johnny asked anxiously. "Are you sure that this is what you want?"

"Very sure, my dear," she said.

"Well, bravo, then!" Johnny cried, and heartily bussed the bride on her cheek. "I wish you all the best, Mrs. Brown."

"As do I," Meg added warmly.

"Thank you both," Patsy said. "And thank you, Lady Carstairs, for allowing me to intrude on you. Goodbye!" Patsy smiled, and was gone.

"Isn't life full of surprises, though?" Johnny remarked.

"Are you sorry, Johnny?" Meg asked softly.

Johnny thought for a moment, then shook his head. "I'm not," he said. "Patsy was very good to me, and I could wish nothing more for her than to be happily settled with a man she respects." He grinned crookedly at Meg. "And, truth to tell, it will be nice to be footloose and fancy free again, I think!"

For the third time, Winters entered the drawing-room. "Another caller, my lady, Miss Margaret," he said.

Johnny slapped himself on the forehead. "Dashed if it didn't fly right out of my mind, though!" he exclaimed. "Meg, Wrendale gave me a message for you—he sends you his warmest compliments, and hopes that it will be convenient for him to call on you today." Johnny winked slyly at Sally. "My uncle also hopes to find Lady Carstairs at home, as he has a matter of particular moment to discuss with her."

Lord Wrendale stepped into the silence produced by this announcement as calmly as if he were entering his own drawing-room. In his arms he carried an enormous bouquet of white roses which filled the air with fragrance. "Good morning," he said.

Meg gave an involuntary start; she lowered her eyes and did not look up as Wrendale came across the room towards her. "Good morning, Sally, Johnny. How's your leg, halfling?" he asked, never taking his eyes from Meg.

"Oh, tolerably well," Johnny said blandly. Sally just watched, speculation written large on her face.

"Meg." Wrendale's voice was a caress. "How are you this morning? Quite recovered from your ordeal, I hope."

"Yes, my lord," Meg said in a low voice. She clasped her hands nervously in her lap.

"These are for you." Wrendale held out the roses.

"Thank you." Meg did not reach up to take them.

"They are magnificent, Wrendale," Sally said. "Wherever did you find so many, so early in the season?"

"I had them sent from my succession houses in the country," Wrendale replied. "I've been waiting all morning for them to arrive."

"You did?" Meg looked up, and what she saw in Wrendale's face made her flush red.

"Johnny," Sally said with sudden decision, "why don't you come and help me put Meg's flowers into water?"

Johnny gestured with his cane. "I'm not precisely sure how much help I should be!" he confessed.

"Well, come along and bear me company, then," Sally said, with a significant look. "Won't you?"

"Oh!" he said, finally catching on. "Yes, of course." He grinned broadly. "I should be delighted."

He stumped across the room and scooped the roses out of Wrendale's arms; his uncle did not seem to notice. "Here, Aunt Sally," Johnny said. "Let's go and find an . . . epergne? Is that the word I want?" He and Sally left the room, laughing.

"Not terribly subtle, were they?" Wrendale dragged a chair close to Meg and sat down. "But you mustn't expect me to repine—I was cordially wishing them both at the devil from the moment I entered the room!" He took one of Meg's hands and began to trace the delicate blue veins which showed through the skin of her wrist. "Were you, too?" he asked softly.

Meg shivered as his warm fingers moved along her skin. "What?" she asked stupidly.

"Were you wishing them at the devil, too?"

"I—I..." Meg swallowed.

"Never look so frightened, child!" Wrendale exclaimed ruefully. "I shan't eat you, I promise."

Meg pulled her hand free. "You don't know," she said miserably. "What I thought...how I have wronged you!"

"Tell me," Wrendale said urgently. "Open your heart to me, Meg."

"I thought..." Meg rose to her feet and turned away from Wrendale. "I thought that it was you, threatening poor Patsy Billington," she said, her voice barely audible. Wrendale laughed aloud; Meg turned to face him. "How can you laugh?" she asked. "I actually considered that you might be capable of the most infamous of behaviour!"

"My poor darling," Wrendale said. "Come, sit down." Meg reluctantly sank back into her seat. "You were very confused, weren't you, sweeting?" he asked sympathetically.

"It was awful," Meg said honestly. "I couldn't think of who else might be tormenting Patsy, yet somehow..."

"Your heart would not allow you to truly believe that it was me, would it?" Wrendale barely breathed as he waited for Meg's answer.

"No," Meg admitted. "But that does not excuse my fault."

Wrendale let out his breath in a gusty sigh. "That," he said, "is a matter of opinion!" He possessed himself again of Meg's hand. "And, if it should make you feel better, I promise to allow you all the time you want to make it up to me—a lifetime, in fact."

Meg shook her head. "How could you care for me?" she whispered. "I have been so very stupid!"

"Do you think that you are the only one that has behaved foolishly?" Wrendale asked gently. "You are not, I promise you—only look at the way I've acted! Blundering about, making you angry at every turn, not even aware of my own feelings until Johnny— Johnny, my scapegrace nephew!—made me realize how deeply I loved you. And last night—"

"You were wonderful last night," Meg said, a soft light in her eyes. "You saved me."

"Aye, and almost murdered a man into the bargain," Wrendale said grimly. "I should never have believed I could be so lost to honour as to raise a weapon on an unarmed man. But when Marden said those terrible things about you, I was so blindly, furiously angry...!"

"You didn't shoot him," Meg pointed out.

"Thanks to Johnny," Wrendale said. "If he had not been there—"

"But he was," Meg said. "And later, you did try to save Marden. I heard you shouting to him to slow down."

"In truth, pet, it was your safety which concerned me, not his," Wrendale said wryly. "I hope never again in my life to be so frightened as I was when I saw you careening down the road in that curricle." He squeezed her hand, as if to reassure himself that she was safe. "Don't you see, my love?" he asked. "Before I met you, I would have said that it was impossible for me to feel so deeply, for anyone or anything. I thought that I knew all there was to know about life and love, and about myself. But I was wrong. You have amused me, angered me, entertained and maddened me; you've made me feel a range of emotions which I thought this tired old heart would never feel again. You can't take that away from me, Meg; 'twould be cruel.

"And I would make you happy," he went on. "I want to give you the world, love! I want to travel with you, and show you all the fabulous things there are to see." His eyes gleamed. "I want to teach you French, privately, of course, and with much demonstration of verbs." He pressed his lips to the vein which pulsed at the inside of Meg's wrist.

Meg was awed and humbled by Wrendale's declaration. Her plans to leave London now seemed nothing but foolishness to her, for how could she ever have thought to leave Wrendale? "Can you love me so much?" she asked, full of wonder.

"I can," he said. "I do! And when I saw you last night, I thought—perhaps you could love me, too?"

"I can," Meg admitted shyly. She smiled. "I do!"

Lavinia Trevore entered the drawing-room grumbling. "What kind of household is this?" she asked. "I banged the knocker until my arm ached, and was finally admitted by a scullery maid. And what do you think I found? The butler, asleep in a chair in the front hall!"

"Well, he has worked rather hard this morning!" Meg said with a gurgle of laughter.

Belatedly, Lavinia noticed that Wrendale was standing with his arms about Meg's waist, and that her brother-in-law had apparently just kissed the girl. "Wrendale!" she gasped. "Whatever are you doing?"

"You must wish me happy, Lavinia," he said, with a clear smile that made Meg's heart turn over. "Meg has just agreed to be my wife."

Lady Carstairs and Johnny re-entered the drawing-room just in time to hear Lavinia's screech of outrage.

"Wrendale, how could you? Of all the wicked, cruel things..."

"I am sorry," Wrendale said apologetically. "It is very bad of me, I know."

"Bad of you? At the very least!" Lavinia snapped. "First you encourage Johnny to pursue that Billington woman, then you lead him off on some wild escapade—the purpose of which I do not yet fully grasp!—which ends in my child being brutally shot."

"Mama, please," Johnny protested.

"Now you tell me that, not content with breaking Johnny's body, you are about to break his heart. No, Wrendale! You shall not marry her."

Johnny clumped over to squeeze his mother's shoulders. "My body is fine," he said. "And so is my heart!" He smiled hugely at Wrendale. "Congratulations, Wren!"

Wrendale clapped his nephew on the shoulder; Sally hurried over, tears in her eyes, and Meg smiled brilliantly. Lavinia scowled for a moment or two, then began to look thoughtful.

"Actually, Wren, things have worked out perfectly," Johnny said, some time later. "Patsy is happily settled, Meg looks to be positively dizzy with joy, and I'm still free! There'll be no bride for me this Season."

At that moment, Lavinia spoke. "Johnny, dear," she said, "there's a young lady, just come to Town…"

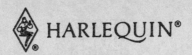

HARLEQUIN®

THE TAGGARTS OF TEXAS!

Harlequin's Ruth Jean Dale brings you
THE TAGGARTS OF TEXAS!

Those Taggart men—strong, sexy and hard to resist...

You've met Jesse James Taggart in FIREWORKS!
Harlequin Romance #3205 (July 1992)

Now meet Trey Smith—he's THE RED-BLOODED YANKEE!
Harlequin Temptation #413 (October 1992)

Then there's Daniel Boone Taggart in SHOWDOWN!
Harlequin Romance #3242 (January 1993)

And finally the Taggarts who started it all—in LEGEND!
Harlequin Historical #168 (April 1993)

Read all the Taggart romances!
Meet all the Taggart men!

Available wherever Harlequin books are sold.

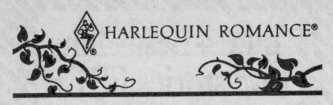

HARLEQUIN ROMANCE®

**Harlequin Romance
invites you to a
celebrity wedding—or is it?**

Find out in Bethany Campbell's
ONLY MAKE-BELIEVE (#3230),
the November title in

THE BRIDAL COLLECTION

THE BRIDE was pretending.
THE GROOM was, too.
BUT THE WEDDING was real—the second time!

Available this month (October)
in The Bridal Collection
TO LOVE AND PROTECT
by Kate Denton
Harlequin Romance #3223

Wherever Harlequin Books are sold.

WED-7

HARLEQUIN SUPERROMANCE®

A PLACE IN HER HEART...

Somewhere deep in the heart of every grown woman is the little girl she used to be....

In September, October and November 1992, the world of childhood and the world of love collide in six very special romance titles. Follow these six special heroines as they discover the sometimes heart-wrenching, always heartwarming joy of being a Big Sister.

Written by six of your favorite Superromance authors, these compelling and emotionally satisfying romantic stories will earn a place in your heart!

SEPTEMBER 1992

#514 NOTHING BUT TROUBLE—Sandra James
#515 ONE TO ONE—Marisa Carroll

OCTOBER 1992

#518 OUT ON A LIMB—Sally Bradford
#519 STAR SONG—Sandra Canfield

NOVEMBER 1992

#522 JUST BETWEEN US—Debbi Bedford
#523 MAKE-BELIEVE—Emma Merritt

AVAILABLE WHEREVER
HARLEQUIN SUPERROMANCE
BOOKS ARE SOLD